Into the Beyond

Part II : Far From Human

Into the Beyond

Part II : Far From Human

Paul James Keyes

ISBN 978-1-952872-02-0

Published in the United States by Verge Publishing.
VergePublishing.org

Cover artwork by Paul James Keyes and Raven Wade Keyes.
Internal design by Paul James Keyes.

This is a work of fiction. Names, characters, places, and
incidents either are the product of the author's imagination or
are used fictitiously. Any resemblance to actual persons, living
or dead, events, or locales is entirely coincidental.

You can follow Paul on Twitter **@PaulJKeyes**,
TikTok **@PaulJamesKeyes**,
or visit **VergePublishing.org** to become an honorary
Chosen!

For Livi,
may this book one day pay for your college.

Table of Contents

Gray...1

Morning..7

An Extraordinarily Extra Day............................ 14

A New Happening...23

A Vague Warning.. 27

Consequences.. 34

Seeking Answers..44

Primitive Science...53

Jellybeans.. 59

Along for the Ride...63

Hard Boiled..72

Where There's Smoke..75

Ultimate Trust... 80

The Cure for a Broken Heart.............................. 83

A Flash of Blue.. 90

More Bad News...97

Fate Is What You Make It.................................. 108

Sacrifice...115

Fated...128

Beyond.. 132

Preview – Into the Beyond: Part III – Fires of Heaven..136

CHAPTER

1

Gray

The starless sky shimmered with the energies of countless universes, shining out from the great Pool of Time like rays of light from the sun in Lewis's own universe. It was a beautiful sight, even within the limited spectrum of vision that a human could perceive. Similar to the infinite depths of the night sky, the multiverse that permeated the immortal realm known as the Beyond was too vast to comprehend. To Lewis, the velvet heavens appeared mostly dark, but to the eyes of the Parcae that stood before him the swirling energies were almost blinding in their glory. The Parcae could see polarization, like the shrimp of Earth, and so kept their eyes cast downward towards the solid mass beneath their feet to avoid becoming disoriented.

The ground they stood upon was not a planet, but rather a rocky plane. Black, obsidian-like stone filled the barren landscape in chunky sheets that crumbled into a webbing of surrounding canyons. Dig deep enough, and one could fall straight out the other side and into the timeless oblivion. Jagged natural formations towered in the distance—steep sided buttes that rose high into the charged atmosphere. It reminded Lewis of Arizona, only blackened… and more alien.

Lewis took the strangeness in without fully processing it. His heart was still pounding in his chest from the jarring transition of traveling between realms. Mere moments before—from his perspective—he was standing in the locked basement of the abandoned creepy house just down the street from his home, being told by Mr. Gray that he was to be left for dead. Then, with all the courage he could muster, he tackled the Parca through his portal and tumbled out of time entirely.

Mr. Gray beamed at him proudly. Lewis's mind was reeling. *He wanted me to go through the portal with him!*

Lewis was one of the Chosen—his destiny uncertain. Chosen by whom or for what purpose was unclear. The majority of people from the mortal realm had preordained paths. They were locked in with the flow of time; puppets reading from a cosmic script. Lewis's destiny, on the other hand, was to be determined by his own actions—of which, choosing to come to the Beyond would prove most consequential. The Parcae could not force him down any path. They could advise and guide him as they saw fit, but it was up to Lewis to choose his fate.

Lewis checked his cell phone. There was no service. He held it up over his head, but it didn't make any difference.

"Did he really just check his phone?" asked the other male Parca. "You're outside of time, boy. You aren't going to find any cell towers out here."

"Don't be mean, Orcus," said the female Parca in a sing-songy voice, "he's still just a child. His brain isn't fully developed yet."

Lewis narrowed his eyes. He tapped into the camera app and took a picture of the Parcae trio. They all screeched and covered their faces from the flash. "My brain is just fine, thank you," he said. He glanced down at the photo. For some reason it hadn't turned out—the whole image was black. He frowned. He wanted photographic evidence that the Beyond actually existed. After deleting the junk picture out of the photo library, he went back into the camera to try to take a better shot, but before he could, the phone turned itself off. The battery was drained.

"Spunky one," said Orcus. "How many tries did it take you to lead him here?" he asked Mr. Gray.

"Many," Mr. Gray responded. "But this isn't the first time we've been here. You two are interrupting my process." He sounded annoyed. He looked back over at Lewis—the boy's incredulous expression demanded answers. "Other versions of you have made this journey before," Mr. Gray explained, "but we've been failing to reach an adequate conclusion. I have a good feeling about this try, though." He gestured at the other two Parcae, "This is Orcus and Adeona—acquaintances."

As interesting as meeting two more Parcae should have been, Lewis was more concerned with the concept of other versions of himself existing. "What do you mean 'we've been failing'? Did I die?"

Mr. Gray frowned. "Not always."

Lewis glanced back up at the swirling sky. It made his head spin with a wave of vertigo. He squeezed his eyes shut, attempting to ground his mind once again. Thoughts of Josie pricked at his heart. He'd heard a scream before entering the creepy house—that's what set everything in motion. "Tell me what happened to Josie," he demanded. "You said the Agares took her?"

Mr. Gray wrung his hands together. "That wasn't exactly the truth," he said. "Josie wasn't taken—she's perfectly fine at your exit point. She plays her part to lead you here quite convincingly."

Lewis was only beginning to realize the true extent to which he'd been deceived and manipulated. "How much did you both lie to me?" he asked.

Mr. Gray sighed. "We told you only what you needed to hear. You don't usually ask this many questions." He glared over at the other Parcae. "You two being here is already causing ripples."

Orcus gestured dismissively.

"Fate has brought us together," said Adeona. "Perhaps this will provide you with a useful set of fresh possibilities."

Mr. Gray considered her words. "Perhaps," he said, "but I have worked much too hard for it all to unravel now. Be gone from here so I may get things back on track."

"May your fates align," said Adeona.

"And yours," said Mr. Gray.

"Shove off," said Orcus. "We were here first. I intend to catch some supper. The path ahead is clear if you must have privacy."

Mr. Gray frowned. "So be it," he said. "Come." He gestured for Lewis to follow him as he wandered farther down the rocky path.

Lewis glanced over at Orcus and Adeona as he walked away. They were already focused on moving rocks out of a divot off to the side of the trail.

"Oow, that's a juicy one," said Adeona as she flung another rock aside. She quickly snatched something up—some sort of juicy grub that squirmed between her fingers. She shoved it fully into her mouth. It made a sick crunch as she munched on it.

Lewis grimaced as he turned back towards Mr. Gray. The doll-sized creature was already well ahead of him down the path. Lewis had to hustle to catch up. Mr. Gray hummed a tune to himself as he stepped gingerly across the loose rocks. Once they finally came to a stop, Lewis began to question him again. "So, Josie was helping you all along?" It was strange to think that Josie's warnings against the Parcae were all lies. He wasn't sure he believed it.

Mr. Gray nodded. "She is quite remarkable."

Lewis began to open his mouth, but Mr. Gray lifted his hand to silence him.

"No more questions," he said. "Everything becomes clear in time." Mr. Gray looked up into the sky, squinting his eyes as he scanned them back and forth. "Just over this way a little farther." He continued walking.

"Where—?" Lewis began to ask.

"—No more questions! I must be precise finding your reentry point." He wasn't the most patient of creatures.

Lewis hated it when Mr. Gray got surly. "I just want to know what's going on," he said.

Mr. Gray continued to gaze searchingly at the swirling energy overhead. "Time in the mortal realm is like a river," he explained. "When you are on Earth, you float down the river at a more or less constant pace. The current of time is too strong to swim against. It all seems very linear to you. The Beyond is like the river bank. Here, it is a simple matter to reenter the mortal realm at any point in time." Mr. Gray's eyes became fixed at a seemingly empty point in space. He abruptly reached a tiny hand into the air and produced a portal as simply as if he'd folded back the flap of a tent. Unlike the dark portals Lewis had seen on Earth whenever Mr. Gray would travel to the Beyond, light poured in through this hazy window. Mr. Gray gestured for Lewis to step through. "Breathe out as you cross—it eases the transition."

Lewis hesitated. Mr. Gray didn't wait for him; he walked straight into the opening, disappearing as he slid between realms. Lewis took a deep breath. When he tackled Mr. Gray through the other portal, he felt like he'd done a belly flop off a high dive. It knocked the wind right out of him. He knew from experience that the portal wouldn't stay open for long. He exhaled hard, emptying his lungs of as much air as possible before stepping forward. He closed his eyes as he crossed through the glowing threshold.

CHAPTER

2

Morning

Lewis felt like he was falling. There was no wind, but his stomach fluttered into his throat. With all the air out of his lungs, he didn't feel like he'd been smacked in the chest as hard this time. The temperature changed abruptly, growing colder as his head spun. Despite the chill, his face felt hot with increased blood pressure pounding at his temples. When he opened his eyes again, he was standing just across the street from his house. The gray light of dawn was beginning to flood over the horizon.

"This is the day we met," said Mr. Gray. "Look." He pointed up at Lewis's bedroom window.

Lewis flinched as the glass suddenly blew out with a bang. In the same moment, the portal he'd arrived through disintegrated behind him.

"That's me appearing. Quick, come hide." He trotted off and ducked behind one of the neighbor's bushes.

Lewis followed him. "Why are we hiding?" he asked. A moment later, Lewis watched as another version of himself leaned out the broken window and shouted into the early morning air.

"Who did that?!"

Lewis and Mr. Gray remained hidden until the other Lewis retreated back away from the opening. After everything that had happened, seeing himself from across the street was officially Lewis's oddest experience yet in life.

Lewis's cat, Melon, was standing in the grass across the way in his yard. He spotted Lewis and came prancing over. "Here, Melon," called Mr. Gray in a raspy whisper. He placed out a pale hand and allowed the cat to sniff him.

Lewis was confused. "I thought you didn't like Melon," he said.

Mr. Gray scratched the cat's chin, instantly producing a low, rumbling purr from the feline. "I didn't back now, but *now* now we have come to an understanding before."

Lewis blinked several times.

Mr. Gray continued, "I traveled back before now and watched you for some time in your past after our first meeting." He gestured up towards the broken window. "I needed to understand you better again after some changes to the timeline. Humans can be so volatile. Melon was very helpful." He stepped up to Melon's side and used the cat's collar as a handhold to pull himself up onto his back. "Follow me," he said. He pressed in with his heels and Melon started walking down the sidewalk with his tail held high in the air.

This must be why Melon was so friendly to Mr. Gray that first day. Later today....

He needed to reorient his sense of time.

Melon trotted down the block with Mr. Gray riding him like a horse. Lewis was barely able to keep up with the unlikely duo. When Melon came to a stop they were standing in front of the creepy house. Mr. Gray dismounted and patted Melon on the head before sending him off, back home by himself.

Mr. Gray proceeded on foot down the side of the creepy house. "I have something for you," he said. "Or more specifically, you leave something for yourself here." Mr. Gray pointed over to where a broken board formed a gap in the rotten fence. "It's in a time pocket." He took in Lewis's confused expression. "To follow the same metaphor as before, time pockets are like eddies in the river of time. They exist within the mortal realm but are outside of time as you know it. Humans cannot see them—not without special tools anyway— but my kind can spot them easily. Go ahead, put your hand in." He gestured towards the broken slat.

Lewis squatted down next to the gap. He felt hesitant. He didn't like the idea of shoving his hand into a random hole— especially one that existed outside of time.

"Don't worry," said Mr. Gray, "there probably aren't any spiders in there."

Lewis paused with his arm stretched out and turned towards Mr. Gray. "Why would you even say that!? Now all I can think about is spiders!"

A boisterous giggle escaped Mr. Gray throat. "I did find a lost badger in a time pocket once."

Lewis couldn't help but crack a smile. "Did you help him find his way home?"

"Oh, no," said Mr. Gray. "Orcus ate him."

Lewis clenched his teeth, his smile fading.

"Hurry, now," said Mr. Gray. "We don't have all year."

Lewis reached towards the fence again. He did his best to ignore the twinge of nervousness that pinched at his insides. As soon as his hand crossed the plane of the barrier his fingers vanished into thin air, completely invisible.

"Deeper," said Mr. Gray.

Lewis groped around as he reached deeper into the time pocket. It wasn't until his arm was all the way in to his elbow that he felt something other than dirt.

"Pull it out."

Lewis grabbed onto the object and pulled it back through the fence. A leather-bound journal appeared as his hand reemerged.

"That contains notes that you thought would have been helpful on your previous attempts at the journey ahead."

Previous attempts…? "How many times—?"

"—Give me your cell phone," interrupted Mr. Gray.

Lewis narrowed his eyes. "It's dead," he said as he took it out of his pocket.

"I know," said Mr. Gray. He snatched it out of his hand. "I'm going to swap it later with the other Lewis's." Mr. Gray started walking away.

So that's why it was dead on the first day of school and already had Kenzie's number in it!

"Where are you going now?" he asked.

Mr. Gray didn't turn around. "I must depart for some time. There is much preparation to be done."

Lewis scratched his head. "Well, what am I supposed to do? I can't exactly go home—I'm already there!"

"Of course not. Don't be silly," said Mr. Gray. "That would be disastrous. You stay here." He pointed at the creepy house. "Read your notes. You explain what must happen." He tugged at an invisible seam in reality and created another portal. He turned back towards Lewis and shot him a little wink before stepping backwards through the opening and leaving Lewis all alone.

Odd little guy. Lewis glanced around, unsure what to do with himself. *I guess I go inside....* He wasn't looking forward to the climb through the broken window again—his ribs were still badly bruised from the beating Landon and Andrew gave him. He walked over to the window anyway and, to his dismay, found it boarded up. He proceeded to search around the entire house looking for another entry point, but every window and door was fully secured. The sun was starting its rise above the horizon. People in the neighborhood would soon be waking up and heading to work. He needed to break into the house before anyone spotted him.

With a broken piece of the dilapidated fence as a pry-bar, Lewis ripped the boards free one at a time from the window until it was left looking just as he remembered it before going to the Beyond. He climbed inside, being much more careful this time not to injure his ribs any worse. His shoes crunched across the broken glass that littered the empty dining room. He made his way to the front of the house, passing the doorway that led to the basement. Gritting his teeth, he eyed the door with a dark glower. He had truly believed he was going to die down there.

Once in the foyer, he sat down on the bottom step of the staircase that led up to the second story.

The journal from the time pocket called to him with its mysterious origins. He held it in his hands, feeling the residual heat of the leather. The pages felt thin as he flipped through them. The journal was tattered and worn out, but the binding still held strong. There was just enough light coming in through the entryway windows to illuminate the words. Turning to the first passage, he recognized the handwriting immediately. It was his own, written in faded pencil:

"Hello, me…" the passage read, "I'll do my best not to sound like Mr. Gray. Hopefully this won't be too confusing. There are some things you must do. I've already done them, and trust me, even though some will sound like the worst ideas ever, I need you to do everything I write down exactly as I describe. It will all turn out for the best. Trust these words over everything else, even over Mr. Gray if it comes down to that."

A note written in a blue pen but still his handwriting was scribbled in the margin and between several lines. "#2 here, I've made some changes. Ignore everything that's been crossed out and follow my new instructions. Things may have worked for #1, but either I didn't follow his (My? Our?) instructions well enough from his description or else external forces have made changes to the timeline that he did not account for. If you screw up, amend this journal and place it back in the time pocket. Good luck!"

The writing changed back to the faded pencil. "Do not read ahead. I've written different entries with tasks that must be completed before reading on to the next. Only read the current entry or else things may get too confusing."

The blue pen scribbled between the lines again. "Good advice. Take it one step at a time. It's tempting to read ahead, but DON'T!"

In pencil: "For simplicity, I will refer to the original me that is living in our house and just met Mr. Gray as Prime." Added in blue pen: "or just P. Short on space sometimes."

Lewis could already tell this wasn't going to be simple. Without actually reading anything, he flipped through the pages again. There was definitely more than just pencil and blue pen written across some of the pages.

How many times has this journal passed through my hands…?

He flipped back to the beginning and continued reading where he'd left off: "Entry 1: Today is Prime's first day of school. You need to go meet Josie at her house one hour before school. ~~Tell her everything and have her read the next page so that she trusts you.~~" In blue: "She knows more than she ever let on. She's on your side. Don't question her. Just tell her today is the day she's been waiting for and get ready for the ride of your life!"

CHAPTER

3

An Extraordinarily Extra Day

The next page of the journal was torn out. Whatever he'd originally wanted to show Josie to get her to trust him was gone forever. If Blue Pen was right, it wasn't Josie who would be needing convincing—it was himself.

"<u>Trust Josie</u>." The journal emphasized the point with several underlines written at different times with different pens. "I know you feel lied to, but it was just the way things had to be. Try not to hold it against Josie, or Gray for that matter."

That was easier said than done. There was a delicate game being played out. Lewis felt like a pawn. It was difficult to even trust his own words. *What if I was tricked again, or forced to write this?* There was no certainty.

The journal told him to wait until meeting with Josie before reading on. He did as he was instructed. He waited until one hour before the start of school like the entry told him and then headed off to Josie's house on foot. He could see his breath in the morning air. The sidewalk was slick with a pale frost crystallized across its surface. He wished he had a coat instead of just his old blue hoodie. He'd forgotten just how cold the morning of the first day of school had been.

In an attempt to stay warm, he walked as briskly as he dared down the slick sidewalk. His hands grew numb in his pockets by the time he reached Josie's house. He pulled out a numb fist to knock on the front door, but Josie opened it before he had a chance. Her sad eyes, deep brown like espresso, glistened slightly as the cold air struck her face. Her forehead wrinkled as a smile appeared on her lips. Without words, she grabbed him in a tight hug and laid her head against his shoulder. She melted in his arms as he returned the hug, though he didn't quite understand the warm greeting. Her soft hair brushed up against his chin. The earthy scent he remembered mingled with a mixture of lilac and rose in his nostrils.

"Sorry," said Josie, pulling away abruptly.

"I guess you already know who I am… were you expecting me?" asked Lewis.

"Yes and no," said Josie. "I knew you would come one day, but I didn't know it would be today until I saw you walking up to the house as I glanced out the window."

"Well, today's the day you've been waiting for," said Lewis, repeating the journal's words.

The grin on Josie's face grew even brighter. "Come in, come in," she said. "It's freezing out there!" She opened the door farther and stepped aside so Lewis could enter.

He shuffled inside, rubbing his hands together to try to restore some blood flow to his chilled limbs. "It's way too cold. I've never felt a September morning quite this frosty," he said.

Josie grimaced. "It's the Agares," she said. "When they steal energy from a timeline, everything gets cold. The whole universe will become frozen and sterile by the time they snip it entirely. Everything dead and still across all time." Josie led him up the stairs to her bedroom.

It seemed a bit extreme of a conclusion to jump to from just a chilly morning, but Lewis needed to trust her, apparently. Still, he couldn't help but question the logic. "If this was the Agares taking energy from across all time, wouldn't our memories of every other day be just as cold?"

"Ever heard of the ice age?" asked Josie.

Lewis narrowed his eyes incredulously.

"Maybe it hadn't always been so cold," she said. "You're new at understanding these things."

Don't question her.

"The Agares sustain themselves with our energy. In the end everything will freeze over, but an unusual day like today means they are here in our realm, right now, searching for us."

Lewis remembered what Mr. Gray told him about the Agares. To snip a timeline, they had to first destroy all of the Chosen so that the timeline would become fixed. Killing the Chosen was the death of possibility. The death of hope.

As Lewis stepped into Josie's room he quickly scanned his eyes across the wall beside the door where the message, "Fate is what you make it," would eventually be scrawled in blood. Right now everything was in its place—a vanity with makeup brushes and pallets all lined up in a neat row; a bed made nicely with a pair of decorative pillows with pink frills at its head; a dresser decorated with an arrangement of candles, framed photographs, and other keepsakes. Everything would end up overturned and broken, blood smeared all over the place. Mr. Gray said Josie was just fine when Lewis left for the Beyond, but he couldn't imagine Josie smashing her own possessions to the floor so callously.

Whose blood ends up on those sheets?

"You have something to show me?" asked Josie.

"Ah, yeah," said Lewis, retrieving the leather-bound journal from his hoodie pocket. Technically the journal hadn't said anything about having Josie read it with him, but he sat down on the edge of the bed beside her and opened it to the beginning.

Josie's eyes shifted back and forth quickly across the words as she read the first entry. Soon she was caught up and they both read on in silence.

Blue pen wrote: "Have Josie prepare the note to give to you in chemistry about not trusting Mr. Gray."

Josie pulled out a piece of notebook paper and wrote the note exactly as Lewis remembered. "Don't trust it."

They read on. In faded pencil: "Go to school. Avoid running into Prime...."

The entry laid out detailed instructions for the first half of the day. Lewis was to break into the janitor's closet and steal the extra woodshop door key. He'd originally credited Mr. Gray for his quick escape from the woodshop, but Lewis turned out to be his own savior. He was to hide the key where Mr. Gray could retrieve it.

Josie and Lewis headed to school together, catching a metro bus at a stop several blocks to the east of the house. Josie paid for Lewis. He hadn't brought any money with him to the Beyond. He wasn't too worried about running into anybody he knew. Having experienced the day once before, he already knew how it went from his original perspective. Because of this, he felt a strange certainty that everything would work out alright. Although, the threat of the Agares did linger in his thoughts.

Avoiding himself wouldn't be too hard. He just needed to steer clear of the gym while Prime was getting his schedule. The hard part would be avoiding any hall monitors when all the other students were in class. The journal didn't hint at how he was supposed to complete his task.

I already used the key to get out of the woodshop, so I guess I can't fail....

The whole thing was a bit paradoxical.

As Josie headed off to pick up her schedule, Lewis made a beeline to the nearest restroom to wait for classes to start. He stepped into a stall and knocked the seat into the down position with his foot. It looked clean. Lewis sat down and waited with his elbows resting on his knees. A few other boys stopped by the restroom, checking their hair in the mirror or using the urinals before class. Everyone else cleared out when the five minute bell rang. Lewis continued to wait. He figured he'd give it a good ten minutes after the final bell before venturing towards the janitor's closet.

When the bell rang, Lewis was surprised to hear the restroom door open again. His ears focused in on the quiet tapping of feet across the tile floor as they approached the stalls. Lewis shifted back and forth, trying to see if it was a student or a teacher, but he couldn't see anybody through the cracks. The stall door beside him creaked open and suddenly the pale face of a Parca popped into view, looking under the side of the divide at him.

It took Lewis a second to recognize Adeona staring up at him. Lewis was glad he wasn't actually using the toilet. "Hello!" she squeaked, a grin appearing on her wide face that stretched from ear to ear. "Longinus sent me to help." Bending low, Adeona stepped under the divide into Lewis's stall.

"Hi," said Lewis, grateful for the guidance. He'd been feeling his anxiety grow as the minutes went by.

Adeona climbed up Lewis's leg without asking and sat on his knee like a small child.

"So, how long have you known Mr. Gray?" Lewis was a master at awkward small-talk.

Adeona glanced up at him through squinted eyes. "That's a difficult question to answer. We mostly live outside of time."

Lewis scrunched up his face.

"Longi and I have been on a fair number of adventures together," she said. "I know him well."

Adeona's hair looked silky compared to Mr. Gray's. The length was close to the same, though, not quite falling to her shoulders, like an overgrown bob. She suddenly perked up again and hopped down to the restroom floor. "Let's move, now," she said. "Less interruptions if you don't delay."

Lewis stood up and opened the stall door. Adeona walked ahead of him, leading the way out of the restroom and down towards the gym where the custodial closet resided. The hallway was empty. Lewis walked slowly behind the Parca.

The door to the closet was unlocked. Lewis glanced back and forth down the hall before slipping inside. "The key is over there in that cabinet," said Adeona, pointing at an old wooden cabinet.

Lewis pulled on the handle, but the cabinet was locked.

"Just kick it," said Adeona. "Really hard."

Lewis took a breath, then kicked the cabinet door solidly. It jarred against its hinges, but held strong.

"Just keep kicking it," said Adeona. "Quickly now."

Lewis struck it again and again, each thud echoing throughout the large closet with a bang. Finally, the door broke free from its top hinge. The next blow broke the lower hinge. Lewis pried the door away.

"That one!" Adeona yelled. "Hurry! Put it in your shoe before he comes in!"

He?

Lewis slipped the key into the side of his shoe just as the door to the hallway swung open. Mr. Bradley, a particularly strict teacher who Lewis knew by reputation only, shouted at him. "Hey, you! What the hell do you think you're doing in here?! You just vandalized school property!"

Lewis didn't know what to say. Adeona looked calm, but that was par for the course when it came to the Parcae. "It's not what it looks like," said Lewis.

"Get over here right now. You're going straight to the principal's office."

"Go with him," said Adeona.

Lewis glared at the Parca as he followed Mr. Bradley out of the closet.

"Empty your pockets," Mr. Bradley ordered.

Lewis turned them out. All he had on him was the journal and the key, still hidden in his shoe.

"Alright, let's go."

He ushered Lewis down past the gym. They stepped outside into the courtyard and started towards the steps that led up to the main office. Adeona ran behind them as fast as her little feet would carry her. She slipped outside just before the door latched shut.

Without warning, Mr. Bradley stopped mid-stride with his leg extended forward. Lewis ran straight into his back and they both tumbled to the ground.

"Oh no!" screeched Adeona. "Run!"

Lewis looked over at Mr. Bradley. He was still locked in the same pose he'd been in while standing, only tipped over on his side. His leg was stretched awkwardly into the air. His eyes were stuck in a half-blink. Across the courtyard, the American flag was frozen in place as well, stretched out in the stopped wind. Everything was deathly silent, apart from the panicking Parca behind him.

Lewis got back up on his feet as he glanced around in confusion. A bird was floating high above in the air, its wings stretched out but not flapping. Time stood still.

A loud hiss sounded from across the courtyard.

"Run! Run!" Adeona pleaded as she heeded her own advice. She sprinted to the door to get back into the school but was too short to reach the handle to pull it open.

A streak of light flashed past Lewis's face. Beside him, Mr. Bradley lit up in a blinding flash that seared his silhouette into Lewis's retinas. Lewis scampered backwards away from the glow.   When it cleared, Mr. Bradley was no longer there.

CHAPTER

4

A New Happening

Lewis snatched Adeona off the ground and held her under his left arm as he yanked the door to the school open and ran inside.

"What the hell was that!?" asked Lewis as he clamored down the hallway as fast as he could. "What happened to Mr. Bradley?"

Adeona climbed up Lewis's body so she was looking back over his shoulder. "Agares," she said.

Behind him the door banged open. Lewis didn't look back. He focused on moving forward as fast as he could.

"We must lead them away from the other you and Josie," said Adeona. "Just keep running."

Lewis reached the doors to the student parking lot and burst through them. Everything and everyone was still frozen in place. The sound of claws skittering across linoleum behind him put a healthy fear in his stride. Lewis ran through the parking lot and out the other side. He was breathing hard and his bruised ribs were aching terribly but he pushed onward, not stopping until Adeona told him to put her down.

"You run fast," she said. "I am glad for it. The Agares aren't slow." She quickly opened a portal and gestured for Lewis to go through. Lewis didn't hesitate. He exhaled hard to empty his lungs and lunged across the threshold.

He didn't think he would ever get used to the strange sensation of traveling to the Beyond. He fell into oblivion. Nausea suddenly gripped him. He closed his eyes. The sensation of solid ground beneath his prone body settled against him. The nausea passed. When he opened his eyes he found Orcus staring at him, a tiny fishing rod in his hands. The line of the pole ran down into a wide pond of perfectly still black liquid. The swirling energy of the Beyond danced above. Orcus frowned at him.

Lewis sat up and found Adeona beside him once more. Orcus turned his attention back to the pond.

"What happened to Mr. Bradley?" Lewis asked again.

Adeona's face held a worried frown. "He was erased. You are quite fortunate, that Agares was aiming at you and they do not often miss."

A shudder ran down Lewis's spine. He blinked several times. "What does that mean, *erased*? Why didn't I hear about Mr. Bradley going missing my first time through that day?"

Orcus turned his head slightly, listening in to the conversation, though he pretended to not be paying attention.

"That man was removed from existence. No one will remember him. The only reason you do now is because you came to that moment through this realm. You were not native to the timeline. Regardless of who can remember what, there was never any Agares there at that moment in past variances." Adeona wrung her hands together nervously. "Longinus would be furious if you get erased…."

Orcus placed the end of his pole down in a crack in the rocks and turned to face them again. "A new happening?"

Adeona nodded enthusiastically, her eyes lighting up as the wheels in her mind began turning.

"Could be good, could be bad," said Orcus. "New things mean new possibilities to play with."

"Dangerous possibilities," said Adeona.

Orcus gave an unreadable expression.

Lewis didn't like when the Parcae talked amongst themselves. He hadn't the context to really understand what they were talking about. He tried to turn the conversation back to his immediate concerns. "So there was a basilisk there with the Agares. And that's what froze time?"

"The native time stream, yes," said Adeona.

"And I wasn't frozen because…?"

"Because you've existed outside of your time stream— you've been here before, so their innate abilities do not work on you. The other you was frozen, though."

Orcus interrupted. "If the Agares didn't know before that we were meddling in the affairs of humans, they certainly do now. You should have just pretended to be frozen, boy, and they may not have noticed you at all."

"At least they didn't find the other Lewis," said Adeona. "You wouldn't exist anymore, even here, if they had. Come now." Adeona opened another portal right next to where they'd entered the Beyond.

Lewis passed back through. His heart began beating faster before his feet even touched the Earth. The transition itself was becoming easier every time, but fear of another attack kept him on edge. He'd only seen a flash, but the illustration of the creepy, pointy-faced old man atop a monstrous lizard in *A Secret History of Parcae* was still ingrained in his thoughts. He did not get the impression that the basilisks or the Agares were small creatures.

Lewis found himself sprawled out on the floor of the empty woodshop with Adeona by his side. "You must quickly place the key," she said. "We have traveled forward several hours. You will be here shortly."

Lewis slipped off his shoe and pulled the key out. He hurried over to the cabinet where Mr. Gray would find the key and placed it inside.

"Good," said Adeona. "I must leave you now. Longinus must be informed of the new happening. Continue on with your instructions."

Lewis didn't like the idea of being left alone without any Parcae to ferry him to the Beyond if the Agares showed back up, but Adeona was gone before he could get a word out.

Lewis walked over to the woodshop door. A nearby bang sounded. Lewis's heart leapt into his throat. His frayed nerves were making him too jumpy.

"Stay away from my girl, Lewis," said Landon's voice from around the corner.

Oh, crap! I'm already here!

A Vague Warning

"If I so much as see you looking at her again, there's gunna be hell to pay." Landon delivered his threat to Prime.

Lewis pulled his hood over his head and ducked out of the classroom in the opposite direction. Landon and his cronies ignored him as they dragged the original Lewis into the woodshop right behind him. Lewis circled around and slipped out of the building before the bullies were done locking the woodshop door.

That was too close.

Lewis would have to avoid all of them to keep the timeline intact. He wished he had a better disguise than just his hood.

He walked straight across to the main building and entered by the office. It was still lunchtime, at least. Students were all over the place and it was easy for him to blend in. He didn't know where Landon and the other bullies were going to go after locking Prime in the woodshop, so he sat down in a chair by the main office and kept watch out the window.

After a minute, the bullies came out laughing and headed down the steps to the courtyard, then entered the cafeteria.

Lewis opened his journal to see what was next.

"Go to the chemistry room while it's still empty and read Entry #2."

Chemistry was right after lunch. He still had some time, but he wasn't about to waste any of it. As he stood up to leave, a piece of conversation between a couple of office administrators caught his attention.

"Who was on hall monitor duty this morning?" asked the principal's assistant.

The main receptionist shrugged.

"Gary just texted me. Someone broke into the custodial closet."

Lewis felt a pit form in his stomach. He had to know if what Adeona told him was true. He stepped over to the front desk. "Have you seen Mr. Bradley?" he interrupted.

He only received looks of confusion. "Who?"

"Never mind," said Lewis, walking away from the conversation before any other questions followed. *He really is gone.*

Lewis hadn't truly known Mr. Bradley, but now nobody else did either. He wondered if he had a family—a wife or children—and what might have happened to them when he was erased. A shadow fell across Lewis's heart and the only way to push it away was to stop thinking about the poor man. The concept of not thinking about Mr. Bradley felt tragic in itself. Lewis was the only one left who knew he ever existed. He died in Lewis's place and Lewis didn't even know the man's first name.

This was war.

The whole world—all of humanity—was at stake.

Lewis didn't know where following the journal would lead, but it was the only thing he could do.

The Agares were death incarnate.

Lewis made his way across the school. He stuck his head into the chemistry room. It was still empty. He went in and flipped open the journal to find out what he had to do next.

"Entry #2: Get the med kit in Mr. Jenkins' desk and take out the little brown bottle of ipecac. You need to go to the cafeteria and dose Jake Wilson's drink, then go to the library and read Entry #3."

Jake was supposed to be Kenzie's lab partner. Lewis had wrongly assumed Mr. Gray was responsible for Jake's absence from chemistry. The boy would be barfing for an hour after Lewis was done with him. He snatched up the bottle and placed the med kit back in the desk. Landon was probably still in the cafeteria. Lewis would have to keep a low profile.

When he got to the cafeteria he found Jake seated at the table nearest the entrance. Landon was on the opposite side of the room. Lewis hovered around awkwardly behind Jake for a minute, unsure of how to get the ipecac into his soda can. The ipecac bottle came with a dropper, but there were far too many people around Jake's table for Lewis to simply lean over and squirt it into his drink.

While still trying to figure out how to administer the dose, Lewis noticed Landon stand up from his table across the way and start walking towards him. Lewis turned away from Landon, keeping his hoodie drawn while also trying to appear as inconspicuous as possible.

He didn't see me, did he?

He dared one more glance back. Landon was still coming his way. He was almost upon him!

Lewis spun back around about to flee the cafeteria entirely, but before he could make a move, Landon stopped short and grabbed Jake from behind instead, choking the boy in an awkward headlock.

"What the heck, man?" Jake cried out as Landon pulled him up out of his seat.

They wrestled back and forth for a second, Landon remaining in his position of dominance over Jake.

"Dude, quit it!" Jake gasped.

Lewis knew what he had to do. With all eyes on the shuffling pair, Lewis drew the ipecac bottle out of his pocket and unscrewed the dropper lid. He filled the clear tube with the liquid, then quickly leaned over the table and squirted a heavy dose directly into the soda can. No one noticed a thing. They were all too busy watching Jake get yanked around between the tables.

It was a serendipitous moment, Landon providing the distraction Lewis so desperately needed.

Landon let Jake go a moment later, just as Lewis slinked away from the scene.

"It was just a joke," said Landon. "Don't be so butthurt."

Not wanting to tempt fate, Lewis ducked out of the cafeteria as soon as he saw Jake sit back down and take a large gulp from the tainted can. He felt invincible. His heart was still pounding with adrenaline as he made his way to the library.

He sat down at an empty table, still smiling to himself at his own boldness as he opened up the journal.

"Entry #3: Wait for Josie to arrive and then read this entry together."

Lewis pursed his lips as he shut the journal again. He was anxious to read on. He glanced over at the library's main entrance. Fortunately, Josie didn't make him wait. Within seconds, she came bouncing in through the door. She didn't notice him at first, but he managed to get her attention with a vigorous wave of his arm. Judging from the surprised look on her face, she hadn't known they were preordained to have a meeting either. Josie sat down beside him, placing her backpack at her feet.

"How'd you know to find me here?" Lewis asked.

Josie beamed at him. "I didn't," she said, "I'm just here to find something to read."

"Huh. Well, we're supposed to read this together," said Lewis, quickly flipping back to the third entry.

The page was heavily edited by a black pen. Much of the original entry was illegible from being heavily scratched out. The black pen wrote: "Don't worry about all the edits. Just follow along. This journal has been through different versions of our hands more times than even I know. Good luck, me, and my sweet Josie."

Lewis's face grew hot. He knew he was blushing, which only made him blush harder. He glanced up at Josie, whose eyes grew slightly larger as she read the words. She didn't look up, though, so they each continued reading in silence.

"There is a book in this library that is not actually a library book. It has been left for you to find now so that Josie may give it to P later tonight. *A Secret History of Parcae*. It is located in the farthest back corner of the library, on its side, hidden within a fake cover labeled *A Contemporary Guide to Cross-Stitching*. Go retrieve it and have Josie hold onto it until she meets with Prime, then read on in this journal alone, Lewis."

Josie remained quiet when they finished reading. Lewis didn't think her silence had anything to do with the anti-noise policy of the library. Lewis was unsure whether or not he should bring up the "my sweet Josie" part ever again.

The warning bell rang for fifth period. Josie jumped up. "Hurry, let's find it now. I have to get to class."

"I know, Chemistry," said Lewis. "Don't worry. You make it there before I do."

Josie laughed softly and shook her head. He realized he was sounding like Mr. Gray. Lewis got up and followed her through the stacks to the back corner of the library. Josie found the hidden book quickly. It was the only one down on its side. Lewis wondered momentarily who'd left it there for them to find, but questions like that were unanswerable. Everything was so intricately orchestrated by Mr. Gray and all the past versions of himself that it was mind boggling.

Josie knelt down and slipped the book into her backpack. When she was finished zipping it shut she peered up at Lewis, her wide eyes filled with worry.

"What's wrong?" he asked.

"I'm sorry," said Josie, "I read ahead through the last part of the entry that was supposed to be just for you." She put her backpack over her shoulder as she stood up again. "Just… please be careful." She ran out of the library before Lewis could rein her back.

The entry must have spooked her. Lewis flipped open the journal. He needed to know, now, what it said.

"Alright. Real talk time. I don't want Josie reading this part because it would only worry her. You need to be aware, though, that the Agares are trying to track you down before you can complete the tasks in this journal. So far, Gray has managed to mix things up enough that I've avoided any run-ins with them. If that is NOT the case for you, and you still exist (duh), then this is our last chance to get things right. Once they track us down, a reset will only leave us more vulnerable. Here's some advice from a friend you no longer know: Pretend to freeze, and DON'T move after the first one passes. They always come in pairs."

CHAPTER

6

Consequences

Lewis had to stop reading. A pressure was rising inside of him. He didn't understand what was happening at first; his breathing kept growing faster and it took all the effort he could muster not to scream. Waves of anxiety washed through him. He felt like he couldn't breathe.

A freakin' panic attack….

He rushed to the door that exited out into the courtyard, but one look outside reminded him of Mr. Bradley's demise. The Agares were somewhere out there. Overwhelming fear and dread filled his body. He cowered down between the stacks of books and clutched his head between his hands.

Panic like this was a new experience for him. He wasn't a fan.

I need to breathe slower….

He started trying to push the terrible emotions down, deep inside. It was hard not to think about the monumental opposition set against him. The Agares would erase him from existence, and he was supposed to just stand still and pretend to be frozen—helpless—as the horrors moved past.

After several minutes, Lewis's heartbeat began to return to a slower, more stable rate. He was grateful the panic attack was finally passing. He sat up, leaning back against one of the stacks as he maintained a steady flow of breaths, in and out.

Once he felt he was calm enough he opened his eyes. He dared to look back in the journal. He still had to read his next task. The Lewis's that came before had everything laid out for him.

"This next part will be hard, but it is vital! You need to steal Mrs. Davidson's keys and locate her truck in the staff parking lot before school lets out. You need to hit Landon in the parking lot as he is distracted and steps off the curb at 1:31 pm exactly. Hit him while going exactly ~~30~~ ~~20~~ ~~25~~ 24! miles per hour (too fast and he dies, too slow and he doesn't get hurt enough). Ditch the truck down the street and get back to Josie's house quickly. Continue reading once you are there."

Lewis could hardly believe it. "I hit Landon…" Lewis said to himself.

"Shhhhhhhhhh." Mrs. Davidson was glaring over at him from the front desk.

At least he wouldn't have to feel bad about the damage he was going to do to her truck. Maybe Kenzie was right—Mrs. Davidson really did seem to hate kids.

I'm going to need a plan.

Lewis tried to blend in with the other students in the library—mostly upperclassmen with free periods. He held the journal up but peered over the top of it in Mrs. Davidson's direction, trying to scope out where she might keep her keys. Behind her on an unused stool sat a brown leather purse. He'd be surprised if the keys weren't inside. He wished Josie was still here helping him. He was going to need a distraction large enough to draw Mrs. Davidson out from behind her desk and keep her out long enough to dig through her purse without being noticed.

Lewis looked around. All the other students were buried in books or doing homework in silence at the various work tables. No one was paying him any attention.

His mind went to pulling the fire alarm, but he knew he wasn't going to do that because it hadn't gone off on his first time through the day. Besides, Mrs. Davidson would probably take her purse with her if the alarm went off.

No, he was going to have to get more creative.

He thought about pushing over one of the shelves of books, but the chance of getting caught was too high. Instead he decided to take an infinitely more elegant and simple route. He walked up to the librarian and said: "There's a kid in the back tearing pages out of a book."

Mrs. Davidson was on her feet and halfway across the library before Lewis had a chance to move. Everyone else turned to watch Mrs. Davidson's rampage across the room. Lewis stepped behind the counter, opened the purse and frantically began digging through its contents.

A tube of chapstick, a couple of smushed granola bars, an empty glasses case, a stolen box of colored paper clips, a ball of knotted-up hair ties….

The keys were nowhere to be found.

Lewis started to panic as the seconds ticked by and he still hadn't found the keys. The lie wouldn't keep Mrs. Davidson away much longer.

With his arm still elbow deep in the purse, he glanced up to check on Mrs. Davidson's location and spotted the keys sitting beside a thermos beneath the lip of the upper counter. He dropped the purse, grabbed the keys, and slipped out of the door and into the main hallway in a span of three seconds.

Lewis checked the time. It was twelve thirty-three, which meant the other Lewis was standing just outside the door to the courtyard with Mr. Gray, waiting for one more minute before he was to enter the building and head for the chemistry room. Lewis doubled back before that could happen. He climbed the stairs by the library, approaching the main office from inside, then went out past the theater and woodshop building to one of the staff parking lots.

He began pressing the unlock button on Mrs. Davidson's key fob as he searched for her truck. It wasn't there. Lewis kept circling around the school to the next parking lot, down behind the theater building. A beep in the distance told him he'd found the vehicle he was looking for. He hustled over to the beige truck and hopped in.

He was still early, but he needed to move the truck now in case Mrs. Davidson noticed her keys were missing and came out to investigate. His hands were shaking as he buckled his seatbelt and placed the key in the ignition. He'd practiced driving a little bit over the summer with his father, but he wasn't particularly comfortable behind the wheel even under normal circumstances.

He was relieved to find the truck to be an automatic. He didn't have any idea how to drive a stick shift. He turned the key and the engine rumbled with a throaty idle. He took a deep breath. His knuckles grew white as he squeezed the steering wheel.

I've got this.

He put the truck in reverse and turned to look over his shoulder. Lewis cried out as he jumped halfway out of his seat before being yanked back down by his seatbelt. Mr. Gray was in the back, silently staring at him with his beady eyes. The Parca chuckled. His whole body vibrated like a purring cat while he laughed.

Lewis slammed his foot back down on the brakes, stopping just shy of the line of cars parked behind him.

"How long have you been waiting back there?" Lewis asked.

Mr. Gray shrugged. The creature reached over and buckled himself in to his seat.

It was best not to waste any time. Lewis put the truck in drive and made his way slowly off of school grounds to wait for classes to end. He pulled over around the corner from the school and turned the engine off. He shifted his body to face Mr. Gray once more. "Have you heard what happened?" he asked.

Mr. Gray frowned. "Yes, I met with Adeona. I am glad you were not erased. We will both have to be more vigilant from now on. The Agares know they are close to finding you."

Lewis stared into Mr. Gray's face. "This is our last chance, isn't it?"

Mr. Gray took off his seatbelt and hopped down behind the driver's seat. "We must make this one count," he said as he retrieved a cooler bag filled with Mrs. Davidson's lunch from the floor. He handed a tuna salad sandwich in a baggie up to Lewis, then peeled back the lid of a chocolate pudding cup and dug in straight away with his bare hands.

Lewis didn't know how Mr. Gray could eat at a time like this. He was too stressed to think about food, despite having not eaten since coming back from the Beyond the first time.

"You must keep up your strength," insisted Mr. Gray. "Traveling between realms takes much metabolic energy."

Lewis grimaced. Just the thought of eating tuna made his stomach feel uneasy. He sunk his teeth in anyway and was surprised to find it didn't taste too bad.

"Stolen food tastes the best," said Mr. Gray with a mischievous twinkle in his eye.

Lewis and Mr. Gray enjoyed a leisurely lunch, compliments of Mrs. Davidson. The Parca passed another baggie full of baby carrots up to Lewis while he partook in a sugary soda.

The more Lewis ate, the more ravenous his hunger became. It was almost as if he'd jump started his digestive processes. He finished the carrots, but his stomach growled for more substantial food.

"Could you—?" Lewis started.

"—I've got you covered," Mr. Gray interrupted. The Parca hopped out the open window, landing spryly on his feet before disappearing into the bushes.

He reappeared a little while later with a fast-food bag. Lewis was unfamiliar with the logo—it was from somewhere else in time; past or future, he had no idea when—but the contents smelled divine.

Lewis opened his door and helped Mr. Gray get back into the truck. He reached into the bag and pulled out a strawberry milkshake and a loaded hamburger about the size of his head. His mouth was watering more than he'd ever experienced before in his life.

Mr. Gray sat in the passenger seat, sharing fries out of the bag.

"I feel like I understand you better now," said Lewis through a mouthful of hamburger. "I didn't even realize I was this hungry."

Mr. Gray nodded. "It's an early symptom of time sickness. It won't kill you, but you may feel weak if you don't eat enough to compensate."

Lewis turned the truck back on to check the time.

"You should practice hitting the right speed," said Mr. Gray.

Lewis finished the burger. He stuffed the crumpled up wrapper back in the now empty bag and then put the truck in drive again. He drove down past the school, trying to get a feel for going exactly twenty-four miles per hour, as the journal indicated. He turned around on a side street and tried again, starting from a slow speed and accelerating quickly to twenty-four miles per hour this time. He overshot his mark. Twenty-eight. It would have been a death-blow for Landon.

Lewis knew once he turned into the school he wouldn't have much space to accelerate to the right speed. It was a lot of pressure knowing he only had one shot. If he went too fast and killed Landon, there were no more second chances.

He turned around, going back and forth in front of the school again and again. He was getting better quickly, but he still overshot the speed every third attempt or so.

"It's time," said Mr. Gray.

Lewis already knew. He'd been keeping careful track of the time. He circled back around once more and got into position at the end of the driving lane by the student parking lot. He was supposed to hit Landon in three minutes.

All I have to do is wait until he steps off the curb and....

Josie came running out of the school building.

Mr. Gray rolled down the passenger side window and called out to her as she made her way towards the nearby metro bus stop. She changed directions, though her movement was tentative.

"Hey," she said, leaning into the window. "You're not far behind me...."

The other Lewis came strolling out of the building right on queue. He looked around but didn't notice Josie or the truck at the end of the lane.

Josie opened the passenger door. Mr. Gray scooted over as Josie stepped up into the truck.

"Umm... I'm sorry," said Lewis. "You can't be in here... I need to... crash into Landon...."

Josie stared at him blankly. "Really?"

Lewis nodded. A nervous tingle started in his abdomen. This was really going to happen. "No one else is supposed to be in the truck."

Mr. Gray made a strange noise. Lewis and Josie both looked down at him. "That's not entirely true," he said. He motioned for Josie to crawl into the backseat with him. "We just can't be seen."

The pair climbed over the center console and crouched down on the floor in the back.

Lewis pulled his hood over his head.

He looked over at the school entrance again. The other Lewis was standing at the edge of the driving lane like an idiot with his backpack on the ground beside him.

Landon was already outside. The bully made straight for the other Lewis without hesitating and kicked the open backpack into the lane, scattering school supplies everywhere.

Coach Phillips yelled and pointed at the mess, forcing Landon to pick it all up. It was all happening exactly as Lewis remembered.

Everyone outside huddled along the curb, watching the spectacle.

"Go, go, go!" cried Mr. Gray from the backseat.

Lewis pushed down hard on the accelerator. The engine revved. Time seemed to slow down as the truck picked up speed. Lewis eased off the gas a moment later, just like he'd practiced.

He gripped the wheel tight, his eyes focused intently on the speedometer. He hit twenty-four miles per hour just as Landon turned to face him. Their eyes met for a brief moment just as the grill collided with Landon's chest and his head was thrown hard against the hood. The sound of the thud was booming.

Lewis slammed his foot down on the brakes as Landon went flying forward. His shoes were ripped from his feet by the force of the impact. He soared through the air before slamming down hard on the pavement in a bloodied heap.

Lewis didn't wait around.

He yanked the wheel hard to the left and put his foot back on the gas as he sped off through the student parking lot and into the street beyond.

CHAPTER

7

Seeking Answers

The engine roared as Lewis put his foot all the way to the floor. Adrenaline filled his veins. He was simultaneously horrified and exhilarated.

"Slow down!" cried Josie.

Lewis let off the gas. He peeked back at her through the rearview mirror. She was in the middle of the truck with her fingers dug deep into both front headrests. Her eyes were the size of saucers, full of terror. Lewis immediately felt terrible. Josie's parents had died in a car crash.

Only Josie survived.

Lewis pulled over immediately. He'd driven far enough away from the school already. Josie stayed quiet as everyone got out of the truck. Lewis wiped the sleeve of his hoodie all over the steering wheel, center console and head rests to make sure no one left any fingerprints behind.

While Lewis was dealing with the truck, the siren of Landon's ambulance sounded in the distance.

"Let's go," said Mr. Gray.

Lewis dropped the keys in the driver's seat. When he looked up he found Josie and Mr. Gray standing beside a large shimmering patch of air. Another portal to the Beyond.

Josie held her backpack out, pushing the end of it into the shimmer. As the bag crossed the plane its form blurred and vanished over the span of an inch. "Whoa," she said.

Lewis smiled to himself. It was pretty cool. "Be sure to breathe out as you step through," he warned.

"We're going inside of it!? Is it even safe?"

"You'll be fine," said Mr. Gray.

Josie frowned. "Okay," she said apprehensively, "but I'm going to be so pissed if I end up with cancer."

Mr. Gray laughed hysterically until he began to cough. He pounded his fist against his chest. "The radiation is fairly mild," he said once he was recomposed. Josie and Lewis both gawked at him. He ignored the looks as he stepped through the portal and vanished from sight.

"I've been through a couple of times," said Lewis. "It's just really disorienting. We better hurry, though—they don't stay open for long."

Josie pushed her backpack through with her foot. She still looked unsure.

Lewis placed a hand on her shoulder. "Let's do it together," he said.

Josie looked back at him, taking her eyes off the portal for the first time. He could tell she was scared, but she managed a tiny twitch of a smile. "On three?" she asked.

"Sure," said Lewis.

Josie grabbed his hand. "One…."

"Two…."

They both exhaled as they stepped into the conduit.

Lewis was acutely aware of Josie's touch as the world shifted around them. His head spun as if he'd stepped into a dream. Swirling lights filled his vision, leaving bright spots behind, burned into his retinas. It was the first time he'd dared keep his eyes open during the transition. His stomach fluttered with weightlessness as he shifted his gaze over towards Josie. Tears were streaming down her cheeks, but she had a grin on her face that stretched from ear to ear. She looked back at him, her smile brightening even further as she squeezed his hand.

A dull headache began to form behind Lewis's eyes as if he'd been staring too long into a bright lightbulb. The corners of his vision grew dark as a rush of blood flowed to his head. He blinked several times to clear his sight. By the time he could see properly again he was already standing on the now familiar rocky terrain of the immortal realm.

A tug at his hand nearly pulled him off his feet as Josie collapsed to the ground. Lewis eased her fall. He squatted down next to her, cradling her head in his hands as she murmured to herself and clutched her stomach.

"That was sickening…" she said. She squeezed her eyes shut.

"It gets easier," said Lewis.

Josie leaned away from him and immediately retched out the contents of her stomach onto the dark rocks. She sat up afterwards, embarrassed.

Lewis was sympathetic. He hadn't experienced much nausea this time, but he still remembered how gross he felt after his first trip.

Josie grimaced as she wiped her mouth with the back of her hand. Her embarrassment waned as her eyes drifted upwards, taking in the strange sights of the perpetually dark realm. Her face lit up again as she took in the rippling heavens above.

Mr. Gray tapped his foot impatiently. "Now is not the time for sightseeing," he said rudely.

Lewis rolled his eyes. "Lighten up," he said, "this is a pretty amazing experience for us humans. Time doesn't even exist here, so what's the rush?"

"I'm just bored," Mr. Gray said, pursing his lips.

Josie scooped up her backpack as she climbed to her feet. "So this is your planet?" she asked. "It's so dark…."

"It's not really a planet," said Mr. Gray. "More like a disk." He waddled off a few steps, searching the air for the invisible ripples of energy he used to form his portals. "I see energies you cannot comprehend. For me, it is horribly bright up here on the surface." With a mere wave of a hand, another window opened up before him.

Josie's face went slightly pale. The thought of going through a portal again so soon must not have been sitting well with her stomach.

"How many Parcae live here?" asked Lewis.

"Many," said Mr. Gray. "There are cities beneath our feet." He gestured for them to step through the portal. "Go on without me. I'm meeting Orcus for lunch."

Josie breathed deeply as she stepped up to the portal. "Alright," she said. She glanced back at Lewis. "See you on the other side, I guess." She looked up one last time, taking in the dazzling shimmers, and then walked through.

Mr. Gray stopped Lewis before he could follow her in. "Josie puts on a brave face, but she is still fragile," he said. "You must take care of her now so that she can take care of you later."

Lewis frowned. "What's going to happen?"

Mr. Gray grinned at him. "You know better than to ask me that." He patted Lewis on the back of the knee, herding him towards the portal. "Remember when I told you that the two of you together cause unpredictability? Well, when it comes to the longevity of the mortal plane, that's actually a very good thing indeed."

Lewis didn't know what to say. He knew Mr. Gray wouldn't be telling him anything more on the subject. He couldn't, apparently.

"Go now," said Mr. Gray, "before it closes."

Lewis sighed. Mr. Gray was already walking away. The plane of the portal began to ripple, growing unstable—the final stage of its lifespan. Lewis dove through.

When he arrived on the other side, he found himself lying face down on Josie's front lawn. His head was spinning like a top. It took everything he had not to throw up. In his rush he'd forgotten to breathe out all the way before diving in. Josie was standing over him giggling. Lewis focused his eyes on her to try to steady his vision. It took constant effort to stop his gaze from drifting.

"You just shot out like a sausage!" Josie clutched her side as the laughter continued.

Despite the fact that she was laughing at his misfortune, Lewis couldn't help but enjoy Josie's cute giggle. It was nice to see a happier side of her.

The front door opened and Josie's grandfather, Richard Mays, stepped outside. He cocked his head as he observed Lewis, nose pressed into the grass.

Lewis's face grew hot as the embarrassment settled in. He must have looked like a real weirdo. He struggled to sit up, nearly falling over immediately as his equilibrium swayed like a bowl of soup flying down a waterslide. He dug his fist into the grass to prop himself up. He didn't dare try to stand yet.

"Welcome back," Mr. Mays said to Josie, eying Lewis with a smirk. "How was your first day of high school?"

Josie offered Lewis a hand. He didn't feel ready yet, but he didn't want to look any more like he was on drugs than he already did. He took her hand and she pulled him to his feet and placed her arm around his shoulder to steady him.

"It was more exciting than anticipated," answered Josie. She made no attempt to introduce Lewis as they walked to the house.

"Hello, Mr. Mays," said Lewis. "Sorry, I'm just a little bit dizzy from the rope swing."

"Mhm," said Mr. Mays.

"My name's Lewis."

"I already know who you are," said Mr. Mays. He stepped aside, allowing them to enter. He shot Lewis a wink as he passed the threshold.

Lewis narrowed his eyes in confusion.

"I made you kids some quesadillas," said Mr. Mays, retrieving a tray from the side table.

"Thanks, Pops," said Josie as he handed it to her. "We're going to hang out in my room for a little bit if that's okay?"

Mr. Mays nodded his approval. He disappeared into the living room as Josie led Lewis to the stairs. She got him to the banister before leaving him to find his own balance. She hurried up the stairs. Lewis took his time, clinging to the railing for dear life. Eventually he made it to the top and then leaned against the wall as he stumbled into Josie's bedroom.

Josie was sitting on her bed, shoving a quesadilla down her throat.

"Oh my god, this is soo good," she said with her mouth full.

There were little bowls of sour cream, salsa, and guacamole. The quesadillas were thick with melty cheese and ground beef. It was the perfect meal for post-portal travel. Lewis's mouth was watering intensely. He sat down beside Josie, grabbed a large slice, and began spooning heaps of toppings all over it. The first bite was absolutely divine. The fat from the avocados and the cheese lifted his spirits instantly. He was surprised he still had an appetite after the burger earlier, but his cravings were fierce.

It wasn't until they'd cleared the plate that Lewis's mind began to process the incongruences of his interactions with Josie's grandfather. Mr. Mays shouldn't have known who he was. Prime hadn't met Mr. Mays yet, and it didn't make sense for his reputation to precede him. He turned his head towards

Josie, catching her attention with his inquisitive glance. "How does your grandfather already know who I am?"

Josie's cheeks darkened as a deep blush fell across her face. She stood up from the bed and paced in front of the window. "You've been around here before," she said, "a future you." She glanced back at Lewis for a moment but quickly shied away from his gaze.

"I go back in time again? When does that happen?"

"Doesn't your journal say not to question me? I know it does—I saw it!" She bit her lower lip.

"Wait…" said Lewis, "what happens between future me and past you? What happened, I mean…."

Josie's eyes remained downcast. She seemed hesitant to answer.

A sudden rap at the front door stole both of their attentions.

"Who's that?" asked Josie. She took a step closer to the window.

Oh no, it's me!

He'd lost track of time during their last jaunt through the Beyond. It was already to the point when Prime was here to try to see Josie after school.

He heard muffled words from downstairs—Mr. Mays telling the other Lewis that Josie wasn't home. The door slammed shut. He remembered walking away while looking up at Josie's empty window.

Josie was at the window already, leaning over to look down at the porch below.

Things aren't in place!

Lewis rushed over and flipped the light switch, then lunged across the room at Josie. He grabbed her by the shoulders and yanked her away from the window. He saw the back of his own head beginning to turn around just as he pulled Josie out of sight to the side of the window and pinned her against the wall with his body.

Her eyes went wide, staring back at him as their bodies remained pressed together, just barely hidden from view. Her chest heaved silently against his own—a breathless expression taking hold. His hands were still gripping her shoulders. He released her, but stayed close. They continued to stare into each other's eyes while they waited for the other Lewis to depart.

Josie reached up unexpected and ran her hand through Lewis's hair, straightening out a few strands that had fallen out of place during his rush across the room.

She craned her neck up, inching her mouth closer towards his.

Lewis heart leapt in his chest. He leaned in, allowing their lips to brush together gently. A wave of euphoria danced through his body—an electric tingle that filled him with heat. It was like being lowered into a warm bath. A spark became a flame which quickly spread throughout his entire body. Lewis lost himself; his mind going blank. All that remained were her lips against his. So soft, and full.

"I've missed you," she said softly, her eyes giving off a slight shine as she pulled away.

CHAPTER

8

Primitive Science

Lewis's eyes remained focused intently on Josie's lips. They shined with strawberry lipgloss. He could taste it in his own mouth, which was still hanging slightly open from the kiss when Mr. Mays called up the stairs for Lewis to come down. He felt as if he was seeing Josie clearly for the first time.

Josie bit her lip. Her eyes were piercing. She had always looked at him as if seeing something deeper, but it wasn't until now that Lewis felt he truly understood. He kept Mr. Mays waiting a moment longer as he studied Josie's face. Her eyes were still tinged with specks of sorrow. They seemed to be begging him to remember the relationship she'd had with the different version of himself.

A future me.

Although he did not have the memories she was drawing from, he could feel the electricity between them; the possibility of greatness was very much present. He wanted to know everything—where it all would lead.

Excitement, longing, acceptance, and a healthy dose of fear all jumbled together inside of him in a confusing mess. Ultimately, as he searched his feelings, the growing intimacy between them just felt right.

Josie pulled away, leaning back against the wall. She motioned towards the door with her head. "Go on," she said, a breathless rasp escaping with her words.

Lewis nodded. He wished he could stare at her forever.

It took considerable effort to turn away, but he knew he was being rude by not answering Mr. Mays. He was thankful when Josie followed him downstairs.

Mr. Mays was holding a duffle bag in his arms. "This is for you," he said. "It's full of supplies—everything you'll need, at least for the time being." He placed the bag on the ground and unzipped it.

Inside was a bag of beef jerky, a jar of peanut butter, and a loaf of bread along with a bunch of bottles of water and a flashlight. Additionally, Mr. Mays handed Lewis a cheap toothbrush and tube of toothpaste, plus a stick of deodorant. Lewis wasn't sure if Mr. Mays was simply being nice or trying to tell him that he smelled bad, but either way the supplies were greatly appreciated.

Lewis knew he was to be living in the abandoned creepy house while he completed the journal's tasks. Until now he'd neglected to put a single thought into exactly what supplies he'd need to live on his own in the empty house.

The unexpected assistance from Mr. Mays was just another layer of complexity falling into place—every moment of his life choreographed by Mr. Gray and alternate versions of himself. *And now a future version as well....* He was too close to see the full picture. At this point he merely accepted the guiding hand and didn't bother asking questions.

Josie ran back upstairs. She soon returned with a pink sleeping bag and one of the pillows from her bed. She handed them over to Lewis after he picked up the duffel bag.

Lewis held the pillow to his chest. He could smell her on it. The usual earthiness of her hair was brightened by a floral fabric softener. It was like sunshine in a meadow. He wished he could steal another sweet kiss.

"I'll stop by later tonight to keep you company," said Josie.

Excited butterflies danced in Lewis's belly. "Cool," he said through a wide grin, "see you later!"

With so much at stake, Lewis knew girls should have been the last thing on his mind, but there was something different about Josie. She was like him—Chosen. Of all the people fate could have paired him with, he was glad it was Josie.

The walk to the creepy house went by quickly as Lewis replayed the kiss over and over again in his head. He couldn't wait for Josie to visit him later. He lowered the duffle bag and bedding in through the broken window before climbing up. Once inside he carried everything upstairs to the master bedroom, unrolled the sleeping bag, and sat down. He turned to the journal for more instructions.

"Entry #4: Wait at home base until you see Prime pass by outside with Andrew, Jeremy, Kiera, and Kenzie on their way to vandalize Josie's house. After they pass, leave immediately for our house. Sneak in. Read on when you get there."

He had hours to kill before dark. Prime would be starting his homework right about now. He had to wait for him to go to the party and then head out in Andrew's car. Lewis flopped back on the sleeping bag and shut his eyes. The floor was hard under his back, but he was exhausted from his travels.

Thoughts of Josie consumed him. *She really likes me!* It was somehow a harder concept to wrap his brain around than all the craziness with Mr. Gray. He turned onto his side and inhaled deeply through his nose, breathing Josie's essence in from the pillow. He wanted to laugh at how stupid he'd been for so long, pining after Kenzie.

He began to drift off to sleep. It felt like only a moment had passed when he opened his eyes again, but it was already dark outside. Lewis sat up with a start.

Did I miss my queue?

He hopped to his feet and ran over to the window. Mr. Gray was yet to give him back his phone so Lewis didn't have a clock to check the time. Within moments of reaching the window he spotted a car coming down the street. Lewis rubbed the sleep from his eyes.

It couldn't be....

The timing was impeccable. Andrew was in the driver's seat. Inside the car, Kiera screamed. Andrew slammed on the breaks, making the car screech to a halt in front of the house. Kiera pointed up at Lewis's window.

He ducked down before anyone else spotted him. They would be on their way to Josie's again in a second. Lewis followed the journal's instructions, making his way out of the house and over towards his family's home. Andrew's car was gone by the time Lewis hopped out the window.

Feeling energized by his nap, Lewis ran all the way home. He snuck in through the side slider door and immediately consulted the journal.

"This next part isn't going to be fun... you need to sneak back into our bedroom and set the fire that burns the room. ~~Light the wastebasket on fire and leave it by the drapes~~. **That killed Jenny. Try mixing sulfuric acid, sodium chlorate and sugar ~~in the wastebasket and place by the drapes.~~** *Don't use the waste basket, pour on space heater, place sugar cubes underneath, this should produce a slower start.* That worked." There were at least four separate notes. It had taken past Lewis's several attempts to get the fire right without killing his family.

An anxious knot immediately formed in his gut. He had always known he was at least partially at fault for the fire by leaving his chemistry set out, but now he knew it wasn't neglect at all that caused the flames. As much as he didn't want to start the fire, burning his room was a small price to pay for a chance at saving humanity.

His parents were already in bed. He went straight to the coffee station and grabbed the jar of sugar cubes. From the bottom of the stairs he could hear music playing in Jenny's room. He stepped gingerly up the stairs, avoiding a couple of spots that he knew to be creaky. He silently opened his bedroom door and slipped inside.

He went to the broken window and poured the sugar cubes on the floor underneath the space heater. The chemistry kit was sitting out right where he'd left it. He searched through the various chemical solutions in vials and found the two he needed. He poured the chemicals all over the space heater. Little drips fell down on the sugar and started bubbling. It would eventually ignite and start the drapes on fire.

He turned back to the journal. "Next you need to disable the smoke detectors in our room and at the top of the stairs."

The one in his room was easy. He stood on the bed and popped open the panel that held the batteries. The unit beeped loudly as he removed them, but then the little green light went out. The smoke detector in the hallway made him more nervous. He needed something to stand on. His desk chair seemed like his best bet.

As quietly as he could, he dragged his desk chair out into the hallway and placed it under the smoke detector. He was glad that Jenny was still playing music—it would mask the beep when he removed the batteries—but he was also worried she might come out and catch him.

He stepped up onto the chair, moving slowly so that it wouldn't rotate beneath him. A crescendo in Jenny's music provided the perfect cover for the dying beep of the detector. He replaced the plastic panel and then stepped down carefully. He picked up the chair and shifted it back through his doorway just as a click sounded behind him.

He pushed the chair farther in with his foot as he spun around. Jenny's door was still shut, but the door to his parents' room was wide open.

CHAPTER

9

Jellybeans

Lewis's mother, Betty, dressed in a nightgown, greeted Lewis outside his room.

"Hi, baby," she whispered as she shut the door to her room behind her.

"Hi, mom" said Lewis as he shut his own door. "I'm just going down to get some water." His heart was racing. He wasn't supposed to be seen by anyone.

She approached him. "That was a strange way to start your first day back in school," she said, referring to the window Mr. Gray's portal blew out that morning when he first appeared to Lewis. "Your father is worried you aren't adjusting well." She gestured for Lewis to walk ahead of her down to the kitchen.

"I didn't break the window," said Lewis. He wished he could tell her everything but he knew she wouldn't believe him. "On purpose, I mean."

"I know, honey," she said. "You've never been a troublemaker. We're just worried you aren't handling stress very well. It's natural for a boy your age to have certain *urges*. You spent a lot of time in your room alone this summer, and while it's perfectly fine to handle your business, it's also important that you get outside every once in a while and do other things. See your friends."

"*Mom*!" Lewis was mortified. His face grew so hot he wanted to bury his whole head in the freezer.

"Your father is too bashful to have this conversation with you," she said, "so it's up to me."

Lewis, now at the bottom of the stairs, spun around to face her. "I am *not* having this conversation with you. Not right now. I literally can't do it."

His mother flipped the hall light on, casting a beam directing down on top of his head. She narrowed her eyes as she moved in close to his face. "Is that…" she dabbed at Lewis's lip with her pointer finger. Lewis leaned away but she still managed to get him. She rubbed her finger and thumb together underneath her nose. "Lipgloss?" she asked with a pleased smirk on her face.

Lewis quickly rubbed his mouth with the back of his hand. "No…" he said. "It's chapstick…."

"The shiny kind, that smells like strawberries?"

There was a pink smudge on the back of his hand. "I'm going to bed," said Lewis.

"Without water?"

"Not thirsty." Lewis ran up the stairs two at a time and closed himself back in his room. Jenny's music stopped.

"Goodnight," his mom whispered through the door.

"Goodnight," Lewis mumbled back. He was so embarrassed he could die.

I'm going to have to jump out the window.

It was a stark realization. Everyone was awake and the sugar cubes were beginning to smoke. If he tried to sneak out down the stairs someone was bound to hear him. Lewis carefully removed the plastic covering from the broken window and climbed up into the opening.

The last time he jumped out of his bedroom window he was nine years old and still friends with Landon Mathews. They thought it would be fun to try to jump down to the grass, and it was. The landing was only a bit jarring on their legs, but they weighed considerably less than Lewis did now.

Lewis launched himself off the windowsill, but he didn't get as much forward momentum as he'd intended. He fell like a sack of bricks and landed halfway in the bush below his window. The bush broke his fall, but he still landed hard. He grunted as he rolled out of the shrubbery. There was nothing left to do but limp back to the creepy house.

Mr. Gray was waiting for him on the front lawn when he approached the house, the large jar of jellybeans from Jeremy's party clutched to his side. "Hello, Lewis," he said. "We must wait here a moment."

Lewis took a handful of jellybeans and sat down on the porch to shake out his legs. He followed Mr. Gray's gaze as it drifted over to the side of the property. A portal was already forming. It was difficult to see it in the dark—thin, wispy lines, twirling like smoke, barely discernible in the light from the street lamps. Lewis tossed the remainder of his jellybeans in his mouth as another version of Mr. Gray appeared. The portal shot apart with a crack like a firework going off.

The two Mr. Grays approached one another. The new Mr. Gray helped himself to some jellybeans. "The other Lewis is helping clean up Josie's house," he said as he munched on the sugary treat.

Another pop sounded behind them. Lewis jumped, fearing the Agares. He spun around to find yet another Mr. Gray walking over to join in on the feast at the jellybean jar. Lewis had no idea what point in the timeline the third Mr. Gray was from. He didn't say anything. He seemed to only be there for a snack. The jar of jellybeans diminished quickly as the three hungry critters chowed down like pigs at a trough.

The second Mr. Gray stepped back and gestured for Lewis to follow him. "You're with me," he said with a giggle. "It's time to travel through the Beyond again. You need to do something else at the same time you're starting the fire."

CHAPTER

10

Along for the Ride

"You know, I always thought it was you that started the fire," said Lewis.

Mr. Gray chuckled again as he searched the air for a weak point from which to form a new portal. "Never mind that," he said. "It's time to retrieve your bicycle." He waved his hand and a portal coalesced in front of them.

Down the street a boy in a blue hoodie approached on a bicycle. Lewis recognized himself when he got closer, already returning from the task for which he was about to set out.

"Come on," said Mr. Gray as he hopped through the portal.

Lewis gave himself a little wave before exhaling fully and stepping through.

Orcus and Adeona were waiting for them on the other side. Adeona wore a worried scowl, while Orcus was his usual grumpy little self.

"The Council has called upon us," Adeona said as she wrung her hands together.

Mr. Gray grunted angrily. "The last thing we need…" he said. "Let me drop Lewis off really quick first."

"Can't do," said Orcus. "They want him as well." He pointed a bony finger at Lewis.

"What now? Who's this council?" Lewis didn't like the sound of any of this.

"*The* Council," Orcus reiterated.

"The Council of Three is the highest position in the multi-verse," said Mr. Gray.

"Like the Parcae President?" asked Lewis.

"No," said Adeona. "The Council is no joke."

"Nona, Decuma, and Morta sit on the council. They are legendary amongst our people," said Mr. Gray.

The names sounded familiar to Lewis, especially Morta.

Mortality.

Death.

Lewis didn't like the idea of being called before them.

He shuffled back on his feet. The portal was still open. It would be so easy to simply jump back through.

"Don't even think about it," said Orcus. His eyes were locked on Lewis.

"There isn't anywhere in any universe you could hide where they wouldn't find you," added Adeona.

The itch to run didn't subside, but Lewis followed behind Mr. Gray anyway as he led them off towards a distant hill. Lewis could just barely tell that the hill was there from the lack of shimmer that usually filled the sky as the ground bumped up above the horizon. Instead, a steady glow crested the top of the hill. The trek only lasted fifteen minutes, but with the increased heat of the immortal realm, Lewis was starting to sweat before they even reached the base of the hill. He wanted to ask more questions, but it was clear none of the Parcae knew why Lewis had been ordered along with them. All three Parcae remained stoic as they marched on up the steady slope.

When they reached the top, Lewis's eyes lit up in wonder. A sheer cliff before him formed one side of a wide canyon, deeper than the Grand Canyon. The whole cliff side on both sides of the canyon glowed with a million tiny lights. Little rooms and giant chambers alike were carved into the rock face; this was just the tip, an entire city of Parcae living in a subterranean metropolis, just peeking out at the surface. There were thousands of the creatures going about their lives.

Mr. Gray took him down a long set of tiny stairs. They were too small for Lewis to stand upon, so he had to slide down slowly on his butt.

At the bottom of the stairs a winding corridor led deep into the stone. It was just barely tall enough for Lewis to walk without hunching, but thankfully wide enough not to cause claustrophobia. Other Parcae walking by in the opposite direction paused to gawk at Lewis as if he were a circus freak. It didn't make him feel any less awkward.

Lewis doubted many humans, if any, got to visit this amazing city. It was all he could do to take in the wonders before him as they walked for what felt like a mile. Hundreds of corridors split off from the main walkway like Swiss cheese beneath the surface. Some passageways were too small for Lewis to even enter, at least without crawling, but Mr. Gray remained cognizant of Lewis's size. They stayed within the main tunnel which seemed to stretch on infinitely into the distance.

A clamor of high-pitched voices arose from a distant chamber. The crowd grew louder as Lewis and the Parcae trio closed in on a meeting hall—the Council of Three was in session, and they had a large audience. When Lewis entered the vast chamber, the voices ceased. Hundreds of Parcae turned towards him all at once from their various delegate seats all across the room. It reminded Lewis of a meeting of congress or the United Nations.

As Lewis scanned his eyes across the crowd, the first thing he noticed was the three council leaders—Nona, Decuma, and Morta—sitting upon a stage like judges of a court. They watched him silently as he walked across the chamber behind Mr. Gray.

The second thing he noticed was that not all of the crowd were Parcae. There were other delegations of creatures, most small like the Parcae, though some were larger than Lewis. Several golem-like creatures that seemed to be made entirely of stone stood like hulking statues at the far side of the chamber. The only reason Lewis knew they weren't statues was their heads followed him while he walked.

In one of the rows near the front, a pair of extremely lanky pale old men with long white beards hunched menacingly into the aisle to get a better view of Lewis. They were at least seven feet tall, though it was hard to tell their exact height while they were hunching.

"Those are Agares," said Mr. Gray out the side of his mouth. "Don't worry, though, they wouldn't dare try anything here."

The old men glared at him with dark eyes, their fluffy eyebrows angling sharply as they frowned. A shiver ran down Lewis's spine.

Mr. Gray didn't stop walking until he'd reached the front of the chamber. Lewis stood with him before the Council, Adeona and Orcus at his side.

"Longinus, Adeona, and Orcus," said Nona, Decuma, and Morta in unison, "you stand accused of meddling with mortal affairs by leading this human and others in opposition of the Agares delegation's wishes." It sounded like a creepy chant, the way they spoke perfectly at the same time. "You have placed the treaty our peoples have made in jeopardy. How do you respond to these charges?"

Mr. Gray cleared his throat. Lewis could tell he was nervous from the unusually wide-eyed expression on his face. "I have guided Lewis," he said, gesturing up at him, "but the Agares have not been present at any of my interaction points. I have done nothing to meddle with Agares affairs."

"Lies!" hissed one of the old men. "Our agents have seen this boy flee with a Parca. He was shuttled to the Beyond to keep him hidden from us."

"Silence," ordered the three councilwomen. "We shall call upon you if we seek your input." They turned their heads back towards Mr. Gray.

"Check my echoes," said Mr. Gray, holding his white hand up in the air. "I have not been anywhere near any Agares agents."

That was technically true. Lewis was with Adeona when the Agares erased Mr. Bradley.

A hairy creature that looked like a wet ball of dark seaweed rolled across the chamber floor to Mr. Gray's outstretched hand. A needle-like stinger shot out faster than a piston and pierced his palm. It withdrew several drops of blood, then rolled away, over to the Council of Three's podium.

Mr. Gray clenched his tiny fist.

The councilwomen consorted behind the podium with the hairball for a moment before reclaiming their positions.

"We see what you speak is true," they said. "How do the Agares respond?"

The old men's expressions soured further. "We know they are attempting to interfere with our harvest and we will not stand for it. Any Parcae caught with the humans will not be shown mercy. Reign in your people or our treaty will end."

The Agares turned and began to walk out of the chamber.

"You have not been dismissed," spoke the Council.

The Agares ignored them as they departed the meeting hall.

Shocked mutters erupted all across the chamber floor.

"Silence!" ordered the Council. "The Agares delegates show us disrespect, but this is not a game to be played lightly. We will continue this hearing." Their heads shifted towards Lewis. "Please present your hand."

Lewis's face was locked in a concerned frown.

The hairball creature approached him. "Your hand," requested the slimy tumbleweed with a soft-spoken whisper of a voice.

Despite his nerves, Lewis lowered his hand, palm up, for the creature. Its stinger shot out in an instant, poking straight into his palm. Surprisingly, he barely felt a thing. It must have injected a fast-acting numbing agent like a mosquito as it pierced him. It withdrew a moment later, leaving Lewis with a beaded drop of blood in his hand. The hairball rolled back over to the councilwomen.

They lingered over Lewis's blood for far longer than they'd spent with Mr. Gray's. When they returned to their podium they did not look pleased. "You *did* flee from an Agares agent," they said, shooting glares back and forth between Lewis and Adeona.

Lewis felt a spike of irritation for being chastised for staying alive. "The Agares are trying to destroy my universe," Lewis spouted back. "Would you have had me sit down and be erased?"

"We do not care what you do," they said. "Your actions do not jeopardize our treaty. The aid from our people is what is in question here today."

Lewis still wasn't having it. "You let the Agares make the rules and bully you into letting them destroy whole universes of innocent people. What do you think they are going to do when they run out of universes to snip? Clearly they do not respect this council. They won't stop with my universe."

"Enough," said the Council. "It is not your place to question our will." The councilwomen glanced at one another before continuing. "The treaty must be maintained," they said. "Longinus will return Lewis to his timeline and will then immediately cease all interfering actions with Agares affairs. That goes for all Parcae. Grave consequences will befall any who do not heed this warning. You are all dismissed."

A ruckus of voices erupted across the chamber as seats were pushed back and everyone immediately began to file out. The ball of hair rolled back over to Lewis before he could react. "Nona wished to speak with you in private," the ball whispered.

Mr. Gray looked concerned. "I'll wait for you just outside the chamber," he said, pointing towards the main doors.

Lewis nodded as he set off behind the living hairball. The odd creature led Lewis to the back of the chamber to a doorway barely large enough for him to fit through. Nona was waiting for him on the other side. The hairball dismissed itself down a hallway.

"Hello, Lewis," she said. "I'm sorry for the ruling. The Council must maintain civility between our people and the Agares, but I am personally moved by your plight. I have seen what you have done and all that you may become. Take this," she said, slipping a cylindrical object attached to a chain into Lewis's palm. "It will come in handy." She rubbed the back of Lewis's hand gently and then turned away without another word. She didn't glance back as she exited the small chamber.

Lewis stared down at the object. It was a simple brass whistle, about three inches long. He had no idea what it was for. Scratching his head, he exited the small chamber as well. He hurried across the mostly empty meeting hall to catch up with Mr. Gray.

Mr. Gray was waiting for him just outside the door. He wore a worried frown. "What did Nona want with you?"

Lewis held out the brass whistle.

Mr. Gray's eyes grew large. "Put that away!" he cried. "Don't let anyone see that. It's a very powerful weapon against the Agares!" He glanced around to make sure no one was watching them.

Lewis slipped the chain around his neck and tucked the whistled under his shirt. "A weapon?" he asked.

Mr. Gray nodded. "It emits a high-pitched frequency that counters the basilisks' low-pitched time-stopping tone. It's too high for you to hear, but it's a very irritating pitch for those of us who can."

It was clear the Parcae wanted to help him, but they couldn't do it officially. This was the best he was going to get.

Adeona and Orcus went their separate ways as Mr. Gray led Lewis on the trek back up to the surface. When they reached the narrow staircase Lewis had to lie on his stomach to climb back up. At the top, Mr. Gray searched the air for a moment and then produced another portal. He remained behind as he sent Lewis on his way.

Lewis paused at the portal's opening. "Will I see you again?" he asked.

"Most certainly," said Mr. Gray with a smirk.

Lewis patted him on the head before stepping through, back to the mortal realm.

11

Hard Boiled

Lewis found himself outside of Jeremy's house. The party was over, broken up by the police, but the cops were already gone. He snatched up his bicycle, still propped up against the side of the house and rode back to the creepy house.

He pulled up just in time to watch himself leave with Mr. Gray through the portal. The other Lewis waved meekly before stepping through with no idea as to the craziness that was about to transpire over the next few hours.

The other two Mr. Grays opened up separate portals, leaving Lewis all alone. The Mr. Gray without the jellybean jar shot him a tiny wink before heading out.

Lewis walked his bike around the back of the house and left it there. He didn't want any extra attention directed towards the abandoned house. He came back around the front and sat down on the front porch to wait for Josie to stop by. While waiting, he flipped open the journal to see what the next passage said. Before he could get into it a passing car stopped suddenly in the street right in front of him.

It was Andrew, in his car by himself. "Lewis!" he yelled out his window.

Lewis narrowed his eyes. He hadn't expected to see Andrew again so soon. He had to remind himself that it wasn't until tomorrow that Andrew would help Jeremy and Landon put him in the hospital.

"We all thought you got caught!" said Andrew as he turned off his car and stepped out. "I just dropped everyone else off at Kenzie's."

Lewis didn't want to say anything that might mess up the timeline. "Nope, I got away," he said.

"That was a badass window break," he said. The jock's gaze became fixated on Lewis's journal as he approached. "Is that… Landon's *diary*?"

"What? No."

"Yes it is! He has the exact same one. You stole Landon's diary didn't you!"

"Of course not," said Lewis. "This is mine." Lewis stood up.

Andrew's facial expression intensified. "Let me see it!" He reached out but Lewis pulled the journal away. "Give it to me," he ordered.

Lewis didn't give him another chance to grab at the journal. He swung out with his left fist as hard as he could, catching Andrew by surprise as his knuckles collided with the jock's eye socket. Andrew went down hard, crying out as he crumpled to the ground. Lewis tucked the journal under his arm as he ran off at a full sprint down the street.

Where There's Smoke...

Lewis didn't know where to go. Andrew was bigger than him, and Lewis was only able to take him down because he caught him by surprise. He sprinted down the street towards his family's house. He knew he couldn't go in, though. The fire would be starting soon.

After writhing on the ground in pain for several moments, Andrew got back up on his feet and ran over to his car. Lewis heard the engine start back up and the headlights flooded the street. He knew he couldn't outrun the car, but he could out maneuver it.

Before Andrew could even get close, Lewis changed direction and ran into a random yard. Thankfully, there was no fence. He ran past the house and straight through to the backyard of the house behind it. Andrew's car screeched to a halt in the street. Lewis heard the car door open, but Andrew didn't seem to be in the mood for a foot chase. The jock yelled angrily into the darkness but didn't continue his pursuit.

Andrew's black eye on the second day of school made a whole lot more sense now, as did his icy attitude towards Lewis.

Lewis waited until Andrew got back in his car and drove away before walking back to his street the long way around. When he passed his family's house he could see the glow of flames growing in his bedroom window. A load pop sounded behind him, nearly making him jump out of his skin as a portal disintegrated.

Josie greeted him with a sad smile. "Mr. Gray ferried me here," she said. "I guess I've gone back in time a little bit? You just left after helping clean up the broken window, but Gray said the other you is still over at my house right now."

Lewis nodded. "I don't make it back until after the fire department puts out the fire." He pointed up at the flames.

"Wow," said Josie. "That's so crazy. No one has any idea yet?"

"Nope," said Lewis. "I disabled the smoke detectors. Everyone's in bed. They all make it out, though."

"It feels so wrong," said Josie, "just standing here, doing nothing."

"Tell me about it," said Lewis.

Even though he knew his family made it out alive, a nervous pinch in his abdomen wouldn't be satisfied until he saw everyone come out safe with his own eyes. He glanced around for a moment before picking the perfect hiding spot to watch from—a tall Douglas fir growing in his neighbor's front yard with branches ripe for climbing.

Lewis and Josie climbed up several tiers of branches before finding a seat where they could watch with impunity. Lewis couldn't help but feel terribly sad as his room burned. All his childhood memories and keepsakes, his whole wardrobe and computer, all his toys and posters. His whole life was in that room. There would be nothing left.

Josie put her arm around Lewis. "It's hard losing everything," she said. "But you can start again. Rebuild."

Lewis glanced over at her. He was losing all of his possessions, but his family would be fine. The house would get fixed. Josie really had lost everything after her car crash. Her whole life, gone in an instant. While comparing traumas never helped anybody, putting everything into perspective was important. Despite everything Josie had been through, here she was, trying to ease Lewis's pain.

His heart ached, but it was not for himself. He turned slightly on the branch so that he was facing Josie a little more. "I don't need any of that stuff," he said, fixing his eyes upon hers.

"It's still sad," she said.

"I thought so too, at first," he said. "But that fire is just a stepping stone to better things. Clearing out the clutter. I have everything I need right here." The flames grew, enveloping the room. Lewis leaned in, kissing Josie softly on the corner of her mouth. She turned her head more, kissing him back desperately.

A scream sounded from inside the house—Jenny, noticing the smoke.

Josie pulled back from the kiss. Her eyes were wide. "I know you don't remember us," she said. "You don't have to pity me."

Lewis scoffed at the insinuation. "This isn't pity," he said. "I…. You're something special. Extraordinary." He shook his head. "I can't stop thinking about you. I want to know us. I want to know everything. Feel *everything*." He gripped her soft hand tightly as he spoke. "You're the most beautiful girl I've ever seen, inside and out."

"You barely know me," said Josie.

It was true. But Lewis knew what he felt. "I'm sorry I don't remember our history," he said, "but I will one day. I'm not going to pretend there's nothing special between us in the meantime."

Josie's eyebrows unfurrowed as her mouth curled into a genuine heartfelt smile. Tears streamed down her face. Lewis held her in a tight hug, nearly knocking them both from the tree. Josie gripped onto the branch above them to steady their rocking.

"Fate is what you make it," she said. "Things could change. The past, your future, could change. You may never have that time with me."

Fate is what you make it. The same words that would be scrawled in blood across the wall of Josie's bedroom. Lewis felt like he'd been punched in the heart. Josie was right. Nothing was certain—not with the Agares involved.

"That's all the more reason for us not to waste a single moment together," he said.

Josie laid her head down on Lewis's shoulder, nuzzling her hair against his neck. Lewis held onto her tight as they watched the flames dance.

The distant sound of sirens cut the silence of the night. Soon, Lewis's mom and sister came scrambling outside in their pajamas. His mother was most distraught. Everyone thought Lewis was dead, trapped in his room. Jenny was holding Melon tight around his middle despite the cat's protests. Lewis's father came out last, shaking his head as he coughed terribly. He'd gone back for Lewis.

Josie and Lewis had to remain silent now to not drawn any attention to their hiding spot. Lewis felt terrible for his family. Everyone was holding each other on the front lawn, crying as the first fire truck came rolling up.

It had to happen this way...

It had to happen this way...

It had to happen this way...

He kept repeating it to himself in his head as he watched his family mourn his terrible *death*.

CHAPTER

13

Ultimate Truth

"Entry #5: You need to get Landon to beat up Prime. He didn't see that little kiss Kenzie gave you during lunch. He saw the big makeout session you are going to plant on her outside the cafeteria right before lunch, directly in front of Landon! You need to be good enough that she comes back for seconds. You should practice with Josie."

Lewis didn't think it could get worse than lighting his room on fire, but the journal's tasks were not getting any easier. The last thing he wanted to do was kiss Kenzie, especially not after falling for Josie.

A note in black ink added: "Don't tell Josie about any of this, it will only hurt her."

The second day of school commenced with Josie and Lewis arm-in-arm, but upon reading the troubling journal entry, Lewis was worried Josie would start asking him questions about what the next task entailed. If he could make it to lunch without her asking him, he could simply read the next passage after that and never mention having to kiss Kenzie at all.

Lewis waited in one of the restrooms while Josie went to her first class. They were supposed to meet up during the period break, and then Josie would go to P.E. with Prime. It was just as the gym was letting out that Lewis was supposed to kiss Kenzie. Josie and Prime would still be in the locker rooms getting changed back into their normal clothes.

The restroom filled with students as the first period of the day ended. Lewis lingered in the restroom a little longer to cut down on the time he would have to distract Josie from the obvious question. *What's next?*

Lewis couldn't stay in the restroom any longer without it being weird. Josie was waiting for him just outside the door with her arms crossed and lips pursed. "What took ya so long?" she asked.

Lewis gestured behind himself dismissively. "Oh, it was nothing… there was just a guy… and you know he was sayin'… anyway how was class?"

Josie narrowed her eyes. "Fine."

Lewis began walking towards the gym. Josie followed close behind.

"So…" she asked, "what do we have to do next?"

Lewis cringed. He just knew she was going to ask. "Um…" he said, "we are supposed to meet after school in the green belt on the other side of the field and then read on."

Josie grabbed Lewis's shoulder and spun him back towards her. She put a hand to his neck before pulling away with a disgusted look on her face. "You're sweating!" she said accusatorially. "You're lying to me!"

Lewis didn't know what to say.

"Let me see that," she ordered, yanking the journal out of Lewis's hoodie pocket.

Lewis didn't resist. That would only have made matters worse. Josie flipped through the journal to the last entry they had read together and then continued reading until she was completely caught up.

"You were lying to me…" she said, "using me to practice kissing for Kenzie…."

Lewis's jaw dropped. "No! It's not like that. I didn't even read that part until last period. What we did wasn't *practice*!"

Josie's scowl didn't lessen.

My past selves were a bunch of morons!

Lewis didn't understand how everything could get so messed up when he was doing his best to follow the instructions.

"Whatever," said Josie. "Just kiss Kenzie." She stormed off towards the gym without looking back.

CHAPTER

14

The Cure for a Broken Heart

Lewis had never felt so defeated in his life. He hated that Josie thought he only kissed her because the journal said to. The evidence against him was damning—his own past selves telling him to lie.

He couldn't blame her for being angry. Worse than that, he knew he'd hurt her. All the alternate versions of Lewis were just extensions of himself. They'd experienced different possibilities and twists, but ultimately each one was born Lewis Graham. They were all one in the same, deep down. Some may have been more jaded or less smitten, but they were all no more and no less than exactly what he was capable of being. Just because it wasn't him directly didn't change anything. An alternate Lewis suggested he use Josie and lie to her face, and it didn't matter that the thought of treating her that way made Lewis feel sick to his stomach at the moment. He was still capable of such callousness.

Despite his mental anguish, he knew his past selves were only making him do what was necessary. Kissing Kenzie wasn't about him. It wasn't about Kenzie and it wasn't about Josie either—it was about saving all of humanity. How any of them felt about any of it was entirely irrelevant. Kissing Kenzie was the only path Lewis was given. He didn't have a choice. If he diverged now, the rest of the journal would immediately become useless as the timelines branched farther apart. Without the gift of foresight, the death that loomed on the horizon could very well become inevitable.

A little kiss and a little pain was worth it to save everyone. Save everything. But even so, he hated himself for it. Hurting Josie made him feel worthless.

Lewis waited through class. At the sound of the first bell, he left the restroom again and stood at the entrance of the cafeteria. It didn't take long for Kenzie to arrive. She spotted him first and came over. Before she could even open her mouth to say hi, Lewis dove in tongue first. He just wanted to get it over with.

Kenzie moaned into his mouth. Her body melted against his. Lewis felt himself sinking. His heart ached for Josie. Kenzie's lips were soft, but slid against his in an over enthusiastic, needlessly gratuitous way. Lewis pulled away briefly to remove the wad of gum from his mouth that Kenzie had apparently been chewing when they started. Before going back in, he checked to see if Landon had arrived to witness the makeout session and was pleased to find him casually approaching the cafeteria.

Lewis grabbed Kenzie's face with both hands and went back in. He was a soldier on a mission, aggressively storming her ivory gates. He continued on despite the shrapnel that tore apart his insides, but his resolve was growing weaker with every passing second. He managed to push through, despite the guilt. He didn't dare come up for air until they were both panting and there was no way Landon could have missed it.

His task was complete. Landon was glaring at him when he looked back over. Lewis just needed to get out of the cafeteria now before Prime or Josie exited the locker rooms and made their way over.

Kenzie grabbed his arm as he pulled away. "That's it? You're such a tease!"

Lewis felt dirty, as if he were coated in oil. He needed to get away from everyone. "I'll be back," he said. "Just gotta change. Save me a seat." The meaningless words felt hollow as they left his mouth. He wouldn't be coming back. Prime would be the one suffering through the next kiss.

Lewis left in the opposite direction of the gym, heading for the school's north exit. There were several choices of fast-food restaurants across the street from the high school, any of which were better places to wait out lunch and final period than one of the restrooms. He decided to drown away his sorrows with some soft-serve ice cream, courtesy of the lunch money Josie gave him before the start of school. He found the treat did nothing to raise his spirits, but it did at least get the taste of Kenzie out of his mouth.

A pop outside sounded like a car backfiring, but Lewis knew better. He recognized the sound of a portal closing. He craned his head back and forth along the windows, searching for Mr. Gray. In an instant, all the chatter in the restaurant ceased. The various hums of fans and friers cut out simultaneously as well.

Lewis put a hand to his head, checking his hearing with a double tap on his ear.

Thud, thud.

He turned around and found the other patrons frozen mid-bite.

The Agares are here!

He turned back towards the door and then pretended to freeze in place with everyone else. Movement in the street caught his eye. A huge reptile three times the size of a Komodo dragon sauntered past a frozen car. Upon the creatures back sat one of the Agares. His long scraggly beard was a dirty, yellowed color, tangled up like a mess of wool. He dismounted from the basilisk, his icy blue eyes searching back and forth as he approached the restaurant.

Lewis's fingers twitched as he thought about pulling out the odd whistle he received from Nona, but he ignored the impulse.

The Agares stopped outside the door. He was easily eight feet tall, with gangly limbs and a slender frame. His pointy face looked like a human face that had been distorted by a funhouse mirror. He hunched down and peered in through the windowed door.

Lewis held his breath, too frightened to move. His eyes were watering but he resisted the urge to blink.

A bell at the top corner of the door rang softly as the Agares slowly pushed it open. The creature's body filled the doorway like a spider, his long arms gripping the frame as he pulled himself in through the opening.

Lewis's heart was beating out of his chest. Blood pounded against the insides of his eardrums, filling his head with frantic thuds.

The Agares suddenly dropped to all fours and disappeared from sight behind a row of booths. He was moving like an animal, scampering effortlessly on both hands and feet. The unexpected positioning was an eerie reminder that the Agares were far from human.

The waist-high separator doors to the employee area banged open as the creature moved behind the counter.

Lewis watched as a pale hand reached up above the counter and pulled open the door to one of the freezers. A scrapping sound filled the otherwise silent restaurant—a cardboard box being dragged out of the freezer and then across the linoleum floor.

Standing back up with a slow rise, the creature remained at a hunch as the back of his head brushed against the ceiling. He hefted up the box—raw, frozen burger patties—and made his way back to the entrance.

Lewis didn't relax from his tense pose until the Agares was back outside, remounted on his basilisk and out of sight around the corner.

They always come in pairs....

Lewis stayed still, but he did allow his eyes to search back and forth through the glass at the street outside. Minutes went by, but the world remained frozen around him. He considered moving from his table to get a better look around, but a creak behind him at the drive-thru window put the fear back in his stomach.

Every muscle in Lewis's body tensed. Out of the corner of his eye he could just barely see the window slide open and an elongated form slowly rise into view and then silently drop down behind the counter. There was no sound to indicate anything was happening. Lewis counted the seconds in his head, trying not to let fear raise his heart rate. He could already feel the blood pounding at his temples.

Fifteen...

Sixteen...

Seventeen...

Lewis suddenly became aware of a presence close by. It wasn't in eyesight, and it wasn't making any noise, except that it was breathing ever so softly. The hairs on the backs of his arms rose up. Whether it was another Agares or some other creature, Lewis had no idea. Whatever it was, it was mere feet away, standing still, directly behind him.

Lewis wished he had the whistle in his mouth. If he made a move for it, he was certain he'd be dead before he even lifted his hand. The presence behind him continued to breathe, deep, soft puffs of air, mocking him; daring him to give himself away with the smallest of movements. Perhaps an uncontrollable twitch. That's all it would take and Lewis would cease to have ever existed. Erased. Snipped from the timeline. It was the bleakest of all fates, to never be remembered, to ultimately have never been.

Fear overwhelmed him, screaming in his head telling him to fight or flight out of there, but a kernel of sanity—something primal and full of self-preservation—reached out with a clenched fist and held him in place, rooted to his seat.

You can't move. You'll die. His primal-self said to his body and mind. He didn't move. He didn't breathe. He didn't even blink.

With pounding feet, the presence behind him charged forward. Lewis hadn't time to even react. As it reached his back it turned sharply and crashed through a pair of chairs at the table behind him. It stayed down low as it scurried by the row of booths and then slammed into the main door and out into the street.

Lewis didn't get a good look at whatever it was, but within moments of disappearing outside the restaurant suddenly snapped back to life. The dining area was full of noise as people laughed and talked and chewed. The register dinged and the engines of the refrigerators and freezers rumbled. Outside, the traffic was moving. No one noticed the newly overturned chairs or the missing hamburger patties.

Lewis didn't move for another ten minutes, letting his ice cream melt into a puddle in front of him.

CHAPTER

15

A Flash of Blue

The close call at the fast food restaurant tied several additional tendrils of self-doubt to Lewis's already troubled thoughts. It was hard not to display his internal panic outwardly. He swallowed hard on a dry lump in his throat. The enemy before him was menacing and truly horrifying; an overwhelming opposition. The whistle dangling on the chain around his neck felt about as useful as holding up a pen to face down a tank.

The threat before him wasn't some bully at school. He wasn't facing a pair of kooky criminals that he could thwart with toys in a humorous way. He couldn't call the police, or run to his parents. This was John Connor facing down a cybernetic organism from the future kind of odds. Except that Lewis didn't have Hollywood logic and storytelling on his side.

He didn't have a magic wand, or the force. He didn't even have a computer virus to take down the alien mothership. Nothing he'd seen at the movies was going to help him now.

There was no wacky professor with a time traveling car… except he did have Mr. Gray. Lewis hadn't seen all those movies, but he doubted any of them would have helped anyway.

He walked back across the street to the high school with the whistle held firmly between his lips. If the world froze around him again, he would at least be ready to give it a blow. He blew into it softly now, testing it out, but no sound came out in any registry he could hear.

He continued on around the school and past the parking lot and sports field to the small greenbelt at the edge of the property. He knew Josie was already scheduled to meet Prime there after class, and Lewis was finally coming to the realization that during the first time around when he'd seen a flash of blue disappear into the trees it must have been his own blue hoodie. Prime would be just barely catching him talk to Josie in about ten more minutes. When he reached the small clearing where Prime would soon be attacked by Landon and the other bullies, he was surprised to find Mr. Gray, Adeona, and Orcus all already standing there waiting for him.

"Hello, Lewis," the Parcae said in unison.

"You know it's creepy when you guys all talk at once, right?"

The Parcae looked at each other and then back at Lewis.

Mr. Gray frowned at him. "Please don't blow that whistle when you don't have to," he said. "We could hear it all the way over here."

"—It was quite unsettling," added Adeona.

"It made Orcus expunge his lunch," said Mr. Gray.

Orcus's expression remained downturned and pouty as Lewis's eyes flicked across him.

"I'm sorry," said Lewis. "I didn't know you guys would be dropping by…. Why, exactly, are you all here…?"

Mr. Gray frowned. "We are not here for you," he said. "We are here for Josie. A terrible event must occur."

"Josie must be the one to allow this event to transpire," said Adeona, "or I shall not agree to participate."

"And this must happen," said Mr. Gray.

"Or all is lost," added Orcus

Lewis narrowed his eyes. He rarely liked what Mr. Gray had to say these days. It was always bad news after more bad news.

Orcus and Adeona stood back as Josie's footsteps approached the clearing. She didn't see any of the Parcae at first as she pushed past the branches and her eyes fell across Lewis. Her face dropped as she took in the blue hoodie and realized he wasn't Prime. Her expression soured further when she saw Mr. Gray beside him. It wasn't until she noticed Adeona standing off to the side that her face contorted into a rage-filled scowl. "You!" she shouted. "How dare you show your face to me again!" Josie pushed past Lewis as she stomped over to Adeona.

"Eeep!" Adeona squeaked as she sprang sideways off the balls of her feet and launched herself behind a tree trunk.

"Josie! Stop!" cried Mr. Gray. "She hasn't met you yet! It hasn't happened yet for her!"

Josie grabbed at either side of the tree as Adeona dodged back and forth several more times before Mr. Gray's words finally registered with her.

Her eyes went wide with understanding and she stopped trying to capture Adeona. Her chin lifted up, no longer looking down at the Parcae as she stared off with unfocused eyes into the trees.

"Hello," said Adeona tentatively as she stepped back out into the clearing like a wary deer. "I know this is very difficult for you. I've just been told what must happen when you are young." She gestured over at Mr. Gray. "Longinus, here, has tracked the energies of your realm quite extensively and says your past must happen the way you remember it or the time-stream will divert to a path where the Agares cannot be defeated."

Josie's expression remained distant. She didn't make a sound, but her eyes welled with tears.

"I don't like it at all, any more than you do," Adeona continued. "I will only go back now and do what is asked of me if you allow it. It would weigh on me too much otherwise, even with all this at stake." Adeona gestured around in the air at the universe in general.

Lewis's heart broke for Josie. She had to allow Adeona to go back in time and change events so that her parents would end up dying in a car crash and Josie would be sent across the country to live with her grandfather. There was no real choice. By not killing her parents she would still be killing her parents along with the rest of the universe. It was cruel of Adeona to even ask.

Josie understood the reality of the situation as well. "What do you want me to say?" she asked through her tears. "'Yeah, please go ruin my life. Oh, and don't forget to make sure little-me feels extra responsible for distracting everyone and causing the crash!'? Do you want me to say, 'No, stay here, let everyone die. We had a good run while it lasted.'?"

Adeona stood in stoic silence, staring up at Josie.

Josie shook her head in disgust. "You're going to do it because it has to be done. You don't need my permission. We all know it has to happen. Don't pretend I can change the past!" She threw her hands up into the air.

"Um, well, technically…" said Adeona, "I actually really do need your permission…. In order for a Parca to intentionally derail the original fate of a Chosen, the Chosen must first choose for their fate to change. It's just how it works…."

At Lewis's side, Mr. Gray was looking off towards the field. Prime was fast approaching.

Josie turned towards Lewis silently asking for help. Her eyes were flooded with tears.

The three Parcae stood at the far side of the clearing, waiting for Josie to approve Adeona's terrible mission.

Lewis embraced Josie in a tight hug. She knew she had to say the words, but at the same time couldn't muster the breath. She wiped her tears into Lewis's hood.

Lewis pulled back from the hug and placed his hands on Josie's shoulders. Prime was close, he needed to leave immediately. "You have no choice," he said, "it has to happen."

Josie's expression hardened into a small frown—as neutral a face as she could muster under such heavy strain. She turned her head towards the Parcae and gave one pained nod that took every ounce of strength in her whole body.

That was enough for Adeona. She slinked back into the brush with Mr. Gray and Orcus.

Josie vocalized her frustration with a high-pitched whine—just a tiny piece of her agony leaking out. Lewis leaned in and kissed her on the forehead. He wiped her eyes one last time with his sleeve and then ran out the opposite side of the clearing from where Prime was entering.

"Lewis!" Josie exclaimed a second later to Prime.

Not a moment to spare.

Lewis continued running until he was sure Prime couldn't see him any longer. The Parcae retreated alongside him.

Mr. Gray stopped suddenly as the others exited the greenbelt. "Go on without me," he said. "I must oversee the beating." He turned back around and headed into the trees without further explanation.

Orcus and Adeona traveled off to the Beyond together, leaving Lewis to himself. He looked around, feeling aimless. A tug at his heart made him want to go back for Josie but he knew that was out of the question. The added trauma she was about to experience from being restrained by Jeremy while Landon and Andrew attacked Prime was just a drop in the bucket compared to the knowledge of Adeona's task, but that didn't make leaving her to suffer through the ordeal alone feel any less terrible. He wished he could help ease Josie's pain somehow, even if it was just by providing a shoulder to cry on.

But he needed to go. He couldn't let any of the bullies spot him after they finished with Prime. The nearest bus stop was back across on the other side of the student parking lot. He drew up his hood and walked away from the greenbelt.

Josie's muffled screams behind him made his chest hurt. He looked back one last time as he reached the parking lot. He didn't know when he would get the chance to see her again. She would soon have the aftermath of the attack to deal with— getting Prime to the hospital and staying with him for hours.

Lewis boarded the next bus that came by, heading back towards the creepy house with a heavy heart.

CHAPTER

16

More Bad News

The journal told Lewis to wait for Josie before reading the next entry. He sat back on the pink sleeping bag, wishing he had a book to read or something else to do to pass the time. Fueled by boredom, he eventually got up and wandered the dilapidated house using a lantern Josie brought over the night before to light his way. He avoided the basement—he still felt anxious about going down there ever since being locked in— but he explored the rest of the rooms. There wasn't much to find apart from some empty beer bottles strewn about the gutted kitchen and an old rubber racquetball in the dining room that appeared to have been the cause of the broken window he was using as his entry point.

He took the ball upstairs to the master bedroom and made a game out of bouncing it against the floor and wall and trying to catch it again while sitting in the center of the room. After about an hour of this, he laid out flat on the ground and threw the ball straight up, trying to see how close he could get it to bounce near his head without flinching or accidentally hitting himself in the face.

He managed to hit himself in the face a lot.

When he grew bored of that, he went back downstairs to the kitchen, retrieved all the empty beer bottles, and then set them up like bowling pins at the bottom of the L-shaped staircase. Three hours later, he was completely exhausted from going up and down the stairs over and over again to retrieve the ball, but he'd also worked out the exact spot to throw the ball in order to make all of the bottles fall over.

It was getting late. Josie still hadn't come by. Lewis couldn't stand all the waiting. He made himself a peanut butter sandwich from the supplies given to him by Mr. Mays, and then passed out on top of the sleeping bag.

His dreams were tumultuous. Walking through a foggy field, the sky shimmered like the Beyond. An invisible webbing suddenly snagged hold of his leg. Out of the mist a giant spider descended, furiously clicking its massive fangs. As the spider drew near, Lewis's fear turned to confusion—it had three heads where the spider's eyes should have sat. The faces of Mr. Gray, Adeona, and Orcus stared back at him. "Hello, Lewis," they said.

The spider's legs worked like a seamstress, spinning him in endless circles as it wrapped him tightly with thick webbing. He couldn't breathe. The pressure in his chest grew, along with his panic, until he awoke gasping for air.

There really *was* something on his chest. Before Lewis even remembered where he was, he flailed around, batting at the figure poised on top of him. It stepped off with a slow trod, yellow eyes reflecting back at him with the light of the streetlight outside. Lewis struggled to turn the lantern back on as terror flooded his mind. The creature stared back at him unblinking as Lewis's hands felt around blindly for the dial that would ignite the lantern's flame.

The butane in the lantern hissed as he finally found the dial and turned it on. Flat light flooded the bedroom, briefly blinding his unaccustomed eyes.

"Meerrrroooww," complained Melon.

Josie chuckled halfheartedly from across the room.

Lewis's focus shifted around in confusion. Josie was seated in a blue camping chair on the opposite side of the room, an off-brand can of flavored water in her hand. Melon stood beside her now, tale flicking back and forth. The cat should have been at the motel with his family.

"Mr. Gray stopped by and dropped him off," said Josie, answering the unasked question. "I guess he's been ferrying as many animals as he can through the Beyond and back again to this time to confuse the Agares when they don't freeze. Birds and squirrels and such…. You've been sleeping like a rock." She seemed to be in higher spirits than Lewis had expected. She stood up, leaving her can in the chair's cup holder as she walked over to join Lewis on the sleeping bag.

"Are you… how are you doing?" asked Lewis.

"Fine," said Josie as she sat down. "I don't want to talk about it."

Melon followed Josie over and sat beside her on the corner of the sleeping bag. He began purring instantly as she mindlessly scratched under his chin.

Even sitting right next to him, Josie felt distant. Her eyes remained unfocused, never looking at anything in particular. The whole situation just felt off to Lewis. Josie was struggling, and for good reason.

"I'm really sorry," said Lewis. "It's so terrible…."

Josie's expression stayed blank as she peeked up at him slowly. The words didn't seem to have registered with her. "What's the next task?" she asked.

Lewis rubbed the sleep from his eyes before retrieving the leather journal from atop the bag of supplies. "Donno," he said. "Had to wait for you."

"Well, I'm here," she said coldly.

Lewis sighed. He flipped open the pages to the spot he'd left off.

"Entry #6: Hey guys, this is your last step for a while. This will be confusing for you, but you need to put this journal into a time pocket in Yost Park. It will be delivered back to you eventually. Until that time, your only task is to stay alive. Do not read ahead. Just go to Yost right now. Both of you. Mr. Gray will be there to show you the way to the time pocket after you arrive."

Lewis narrowed his eyes. He glanced up at Josie. Her lips were pursed.

"Why do I even need to be here?" she asked. "This doesn't have anything to do with me."

Lewis flipped to the next page. "Hi Landon," the journal continued. "Your first task is simple. Go to the cubby where we put our backpacks and find mine. Pour a cup of water into my backpack when no one's looking so that it gets all over my binder and papers. Make it a habit to do this every week or so. And Lewis, I knew you'd be too curious to not read this, but seriously stop now."

He snapped the journal shut, perplexed.

Landon....

The last time he'd had a backpack in a cubby hole was in elementary school. There was a stint in the third grade when he'd often found his belongings soaking wet. He'd never known how it was happening, and it had taken quite a toll on his emotional health at the time.

Seeing instructions from himself to a young Landon, his tormentor, was beyond disturbing. He glanced up at Josie. She looked just as confused.

"What does he have to do with any of this?" she asked.

"I have no idea..." said Lewis. He gave Melon a rub on the head as he stood up to leave. Josie followed behind him as he hurried down the stairs and out the broken dining room window. Josie's bicycle was propped up against the side of the house. Lewis ran around the back to retrieve his own. He had endless questions for Mr. Gray.

They set off for Yost Park. The moon was nearly full, sitting high in the dark sky as they pedaled down the street side by side.

"What's a time pocket?" asked Josie after rounding the first corner.

"I got the journal out of one. Mr. Gray said it's like an eddy in the river of time. If you put something inside, you can retrieve it in the future or in the past, I guess."

"Hmm," said Josie. "If you crawled inside one, when would you come out?"

Lewis didn't know the answer, but Josie hadn't really been expecting one. They rode on in quiet contemplation until they reached the main entrance to the park. The journal hadn't mentioned where exactly in Yost they were supposed to meet Mr. Gray, so they meandered about for several minutes until a passing car prompted them to ride down the main drive to get out of sight. The park was closed at this hour, so it was best not to be seen. They dismounted and walked their bikes off to the side into the brush in case anyone else happened by.

Yost was a sizable park by Edmonds standards. Tall trees and thick underbrush laced with trails stretched about half a mile into the darkness. There was a pool facility at the end of the drive, but the trails seemed a more likely place for a time pocket than the popular pool.

Josie used her phone to light the way as they walked towards the nearest trailhead. They didn't really have any idea where they were supposed to go. They just wandered aimlessly.

It was a chilly night, possibly due to the Agares if Josie's earlier summation was correct. She walked with her arms crossed beneath her breasts; her phone clutched tight in her fingers and pointed down to light the path.

Lewis stepped gingerly beside her, avoiding roots and divots. He could feel the tension of unspoken words growing as they moved deeper into the trees. Finally, he couldn't take it any longer. "There was nothing else you could have done," he said. "It wasn't fair."

Josie's hair blew around her face as a gust of cold wind blew through the foliage. She hugged herself tighter and quickened her pace.

Lewis matched her stride, not giving up. "You aren't responsible for their deaths. The only thing you are responsible for is giving everyone else a chance to survive the Agares."

Josie scoffed. "Do you want to know what I think?" She didn't wait for Lewis to respond. "I think I could have chosen to save them and lived the life I was born into and everyone else could have lived their lives too and who cares if the Agares take all the energy in the end? What's the difference between stopping existing and death? We all live, and we all die."

"Being erased—" Lewis started.

"—Death is inevitable. We are fretting over time ending, but we are creatures of time. The Parcae treat us like some mural painted on a wall. To them, all of human existence has already happened—it must have already happened if we can go back to any point in time. Why should the mural care if it gets torn down? I could have lived my life to the fullest with my parents and one day died and never would have known anything about the universe ending or cared about it in the slightest. One day the sun will blow up and humanity will cease to exist, so what are we trying to save? Existing and then not existing is the nature of life. The only difference is now, because of my choice, my parents are dead, prematurely, and they didn't get to live the life they were meant to have. And what do I get from their sacrifice? To move across the country so I could meet you? Would you let your parents die just so you could meet me?"

Lewis didn't know what to say. Josie stared back at him searchingly. It was a lot to take in. What she said made a lot of sense. The Parcae cared about humanity's continued existence because to them Earth was a place they could visit from outside of time. Humans throughout history had already lived out their lives. All future people had lived theirs as well, when viewed from the Beyond anyway. If the Agares snipped the universe, from humanity's perspective, ceasing to exist wouldn't diminish the value of the lives lived. *Or would it?* The whole thing was overwhelmingly philosophical.

There was one thing Josie hadn't taken into account, though. "Do you know who Mr. Bradley is?" he asked.

Josie shook her head.

"That's because the Agares erased him by accident yesterday when they came for me."

Josie stopped walking and turned to face him.

"I remember him because I was already outside of my original time stream by then. I don't know if he had a family, but if he did, they probably have empty holes in their lives they can't explain. The Agares have to be stopped and we are the only ones who might have a chance of stopping them. Did time freeze for you during last period today?"

Josie nodded meekly, her eyebrows lowering into a frown. "I stood still, like the journal said, but nothing happened, and then everything started moving again after a bit."

"That was the Agares, trying to find us again. They keep coming here, now, looking for us, and they won't stop until we don't exist anymore." He paused briefly to let the words sink in. "If you hadn't allowed Adeona to do what she needed to do, they would have found you years ago and ripped you right out of your parents' minds. Who's to say they wouldn't have erased your whole family at the same time?"

Josie's eyes stayed locked on his.

"I feel something when I'm around you," said Lewis, "something strange and exhilarating. You talk about the life you were meant to have—what you were born into—but I don't think either one of us really knows exactly what that even means. We were both born Chosen. I don't know if it's a gift or a curse, but we are the only ones who can choose our own destinies."

Josie breathed heavily, the focus of her eyes flicking back and forth between his own.

"I think we were destined to meet," he continued. "I want to know you. I want to live a life free from the Agares. But the only way that's going to happen is if we make it happen." He reached his hand up and brushed some of Josie's disheveled hair from her forehead and tucked it behind her ear. "We'll get through this together."

Josie's expression didn't change, but she moved forward, burying her face into his shoulder. He wrapped his arms around her, clasping her in a tight hug. Before she pulled away he kissed her on the forehead.

Behind Josie from within a square of deadened air about fifteen crows burst through a portal and into the park, cawing up a storm. Mr. Gray came through behind them shaking a leafy branch, his lips curled down in a tiny frown. "I could only get about half of them to fly back through from the Beyond," he said. Three more crows darted past his head, exiting the portal on their own.   Mr. Gray groaned in annoyance as the window disintegrated.

Lewis didn't waste any time. "Why am I writing to Landon in the journal?" he asked, accusatorially.

Mr. Gray shook his branch at Lewis. "You know I can't tell you things about your fate," he said. "And besides, that journal is your business. I never told you to write it."

So Landon has something to do with my fate....

He knew that was as much of a hint as he was going to get from Mr. Gray.

"The pocket is over there," said Mr. Gray, pointing with his branch at a nearby tree.

Josie shined her light to where Mr. Gray was pointing. A root at the base of a tree poked up above the earth a couple of inches.

Mr. Gray ambled over to the spot and cleared away some moss. "Just shove it in," he said.

Lewis shrugged to himself. He knelt down beside the root and slipped the journal across the invisible barrier. Josie squatted beside him, inspecting the pocket. A trail of tiny ants had formed a procession, heading into the anomaly. They didn't appear to be coming back out again. Josie stuck her hand in, musing over her fingers vanishing and reappearing as she moved them in and out.

Without the journal, they would have to rely on Mr. Gray alone for guidance.

"Bye," said Mr. Gray. He opened a new portal and was gone in a blink of an eye.

CHAPTER

17

Fate Is What You Make It

The next day a warm front drifted across the Pacific Northwest. It felt like summer again as temperatures spiked into the high sixties. Lewis laid his blue hoodie to rest, keeping his gray t-shirt as his only layer. Mr. Mays offered to wash Lewis's clothes during his own laundry run, so Lewis stripped down and utilized the time to take a much needed shower.

Josie brought him a fresh towel before he began. She lingered a little too long in the doorway upon seeing Lewis's shirtless body. Mr. Mays grunted his disapproval. Josie's cheeks lit up with an embarrassed blush as she quickly shut the door between herself and Lewis.

He felt his own face grow hot as butterflies danced in his stomach. He wasn't used to the kind of attention Josie was paying him. Not being particularly muscular, he had never considered that a girl might enjoy looking at him in a sexual way. His unfamiliarity with the situation manifested itself as bashfulness. He wrapped the towel tightly around his middle before opening the door again to deliver the rest of his clothing to Mr. Mays. He was greeted with a scowl.

The following weeks went by slowly. With no journal to guide him, he didn't have much to do during the time Prime was in the hospital. Josie cut class to hang out with him on most days—a much welcome development. Mr. Mays called in sick for her to the high school on each day she stayed home, no questions asked. Lewis still wasn't exactly sure how much of their situation Josie's grandfather understood. He allowed Lewis to stay over at their house during the day, but insisted he spent his nights alone at the creepy house.

Lewis's feelings for Josie only grew stronger the more time they spent together. He loved so many things about her, from the way she laughed—a jovial giggle that always escaped suddenly from deep down in her belly, sometimes at the most inappropriate of times—to the way she cared about every animal she came across as if they were her equal. She cared deeply and honestly, always wearing her heart on her sleeve, unafraid to show her tidal waves of emotion.

Lewis was used to keeping everything pent up inside, but Josie's thirst for life was infectious. She was chipping away at his armor, slowly but surely.

Although he was enjoying his time with her, he began counting down the days until he could integrate back into his old life. He missed his family dearly, and didn't particularly enjoy sleeping on the floor of an abandoned house. He was nearing the end of his wait. At this point there was only three more days before Prime would disappear into the Beyond and he could take his place back at home.

The next afternoon, with his body draped over the wooden swing in Josie's front yard, Lewis mindlessly swayed back and forth. Josie dragged a lawn chair around from the back of the house and joined him in his daze. The continued heat relieved some of Lewis's anxiety—it suggested the Agares were no longer present at this time in the mortal realm. It also made sleeping easier in the unheated, abandoned house.

Josie sipped on some lemonade as she flipped through the pages of a poetry book, *Passenger Poet*. The spine was broken in and the pages tattered from multiple read-throughs. Josie remained engrossed in the pages until it was nearly time for dinner. After all the insanity of the first days of school, it was nice to be able to relax a little bit.

Lewis, curious as to what drew Josie so intensely to the poems, sat beside her for some time, reading over her shoulder.

<u>Vagabond</u>

It is not your fault my dear
Distance calls to you with such urgent alarm bells

Let your hands touch softly your keys and
Contemplation

Let your eyes fix a little harder on the skyline

Unravel the tension from the string
You have spun for yourself

You do not owe your past a trail of breadcrumbs

Feel the weight of all that is behind you

Allow that force to carry you forward

<u>Wandering Heart</u>

Perhaps
The relief of such motion
Came to her not in surprise
But rather softly

As warm tea on the porch in the summer
As a cat at the foot of the bed
As rain on the top of the tin roof

Josie, for all her trauma, seemed more at peace with the reality of her life when she poured herself across those words. Lewis could still see the struggle inside of her, but between the poems and the support of her grandfather, she was already several steps back from the ledge she had been nearing on the night they deposited the journal into the time pocket. Mr. Mays loved her dearly, and it showed in the tender way he treated her; tight hugs that lingered through the sorrow. Their deep bond was the most tangible gain to come out of the sacrifice she had made.

After dinner, Lewis headed back to the creepy house. He only needed to spend two more nights there before Prime's departure to the Beyond. He was running low on supplies, though, so the next day Josie went with him to the grocery store and purchased a couple jugs of water and some pre-made sandwiches to help sustain him through to the end. When they got back she passed the bag up through the broken window and then climbed in behind Lewis. They hadn't been inside more than five minutes when a knock at the front door hushed their chatter.

Lewis crept over to the master bedroom window and peeked out. He couldn't quite see who was at the door, but there were no cars parked outside. They both remained silent, waiting for whoever it was to give up and walk away.

"I know you're in there!" came a yell from the front porch. "Come on, let me in! I saw your bikes around the side."

Josie leaned past Lewis and opened the bedroom window to get a better look. Stepping back down from the porch, Landon's head appeared out from behind the eve, looking up at them.

Upon seeing their incredulous stares Landon lifted the leather-bound journal up over his head with his left arm. "I come in peace," he said. His right arm was still in a sling.

Lewis and Josie looked at each other, and then back down at Landon.

"I won't bite," pleaded Landon.

"The front is boarded up," said Lewis, still wary. "You can use the broken window by our bikes."

They waited in the bedroom for Landon to climb in and make his way up. When the bully reached the top of the stairs he read the prickly atmosphere of the room and smartly didn't approach either of them.

"Here you go," he said, holding up the journal for Lewis to take. "I found this when I was nine."

Lewis approached Landon as if he were a wild animal. He snatched the journal out of his hand and backed away again immediately. Landon put his hand up, unfazed by Lewis's cautious approach. Lewis flipped through the pages, confirming that it was in fact the same journal they'd placed into the time pocket days before.

"I'm really sorry that I had to beat you up," said Landon. "And for being an ass all these years. I was just following your instructions."

Josie scrunched up her face.

Lewis wasn't sure how to respond. "Well, I guess I'm sorry I had to hit you with a truck, then," he said.

"I knew it was coming."

Josie's eyes were wide, looking back and forth between the two boys.

"It says we are supposed to read the next entry together," said Landon.

Lewis nodded slowly. He gestured for Landon to follow him to the sleeping bag. They both sat down cross-legged. Josie crouched down behind them as Landon helped direct Lewis to the correct page—about three quarters of the way through. The vast majority of the journal was dedicated to directing Landon's life.

"Entry #112: Landon and Lewis, what a journey we have all had…. I have a confession to make. I am not the first Lewis to pass instructions down to change the timeline. I have been working from a journal of my own which had numerous corrections in it already. I have no idea how many Lewis's came before. Maybe this cycle is infinite…. Anyway, I saw that after so many attempts every Lewis always failed. Finally, with me, every possible scenario had already been tweaked and manipulated. There was nothing left to do different that hadn't already been tried—no way to win with the current deck of cards, so I set out to get a new deck. I had Gray help me drastically change the timeline and left the journal for Landon when he was 9 years old. Landon is my best friend, though if he does everything I set out for him he certainly won't be yours. I feel terrible about this, but it was the best way to turn everything on its head and give us a new set of possibilities to work with. In my timeline, Landon actually helped me write this journal. Despite your years of being at odds with each other, Lewis, you must know that it was all my manipulation that caused this. You must forgive his bullying. You two actually work very well together. If you've done everything you were supposed to do, Landon, then I only have one more request of you. Be Lewis's friend again. There are difficult trials ahead and he will need you by his side the way you were by mine, the way you were always meant to be, if we are to have any hope of saving the universe."

CHAPTER

18

Sacrifice

Everything Lewis knew about his entire life since he was nine years old was a complete lie. A lie he told himself. He felt like a bucket of ice water had been dumped over his head. Everything he knew and felt about Landon was wrong. He was his own tormentor, his friendships stripped away by bullying of his own devise. He had sacrificed a happy childhood out of necessity. He was furious at this other Lewis, but he knew the feelings were futile. The other Lewis didn't exist anymore. He had failed to save humanity and had chosen to erase himself—intentionally replaced himself with a new Lewis who'd been beaten down time and time again.

The new possibilities cost the other Lewis everything. He knew the decision had not been made lightly.

There was no telling how far down the path of new possibilities his current attempt at life resided, but he knew this was his last chance. The Agares were narrowing in on him.

115

Landon left the journal with Lewis and departed for the night. There was still a lot for Lewis to process. He couldn't simply flip a switch and start acting like Landon was his best friend again.

Josie stayed with him until late into the night. They read through most of Landon's entries in the journal and talked for hours about all the terrible things he'd caused for Lewis over the last eight years.

"Oh, geez, look at this one," said Josie, holding up the journal.

"Entry #53: Buy a can of spray paint and draw a dick on my garage in the middle of the night. Bonus points if Melon comes out and you can spray him too. The more wary of the neighborhood I become, the better."

Lewis frowned. "We had to shave him."

"Poor kitty," said Josie. She flipped ahead a few more pages.

"Entry #59: Take the large magnet from your birthday and swipe it over my thumb drive for the history project after I've placed it on Mr. Carmen's desk. It's the red one with the metallic swivel port cover. Skip last period and head to my house—my mom will let you in. She doesn't know we aren't friends anymore. Just say you're planning a surprise for me. Use the magnet on my laptop too."

"Creative," said Lewis.

"This brings new meaning to being 'Your own worst enemy,'" said Josie.

Lewis hadn't even realized Landon had been responsible for half of the chaos he'd experienced at the time. He knew he only had himself to blame. Reading the entries wasn't helping him come to terms with forgiving Landon for his actions.

After Josie went home to sleep, Lewis laid awake for hours. Tomorrow was going to be a big day according to the next journal entry. Entry #113 detailed the steps they needed to take to get Lewis locked in the basement of the creepy house. Each of them, including Landon, had their parts to play to lure Prime out of his home and into the abandoned house.

Lewis wasn't technically supposed to have read the entry until they all were to meet up again in the morning, but he couldn't help himself. He internalized the directions so that he was ready for the intricate dance ahead. None of them could be seen by Prime if he was to make the leap into the Beyond.

After reading the entry through several times, a nagging feeling planted a kernel of doubt in his mind. A piece of the puzzle of that night was still missing. Nowhere in all the instructions did the journal mention anything about Josie's ransacked bedroom or the message that would be scrawled in blood across her wall. As far as he could tell, something unplanned was going to happen. The journal provided no foresight.

Sleep did not come easy.

Josie and Landon arrived before Lewis awoke the next morning. The heatwave was over, replaced with a bitter chill. Lewis could see his breath in the unheated house. He shared his concerns with the others after they read through the instructions.

"Do you think it's the Agares?" asked Landon.

"What else could it be? The actions of the Agares are the only occurrences the alternate us couldn't chronicle," said Lewis. "Their presence here is new."

"We could just avoid my house," said Josie.

Landon shook his head. "If we don't do everything exactly as Lewis remembers it we'll mess up the timeline and he might not go through the portal. What did the message say again?"

"Fate is what you make it," said Lewis.

"You're sure it was drawn in blood?" asked Josie.

"I mean, I didn't taste it or anything," said Lewis, "but it looked like blood. And there was more smeared on the side of the house before I climbed in."

"It doesn't say anything about that…" said Landon.

"It doesn't say anything about any of it," said Lewis. "Mr. Mays told me Josie had gone missing. He'd just finished talking to a policeman. Her room was wrecked with blood everywhere and the message on the wall."

"Do you think Mr. Gray knows anything?" asked Josie.

"He definitely does," said Lewis. "He was there for all of it, but I haven't seen him in weeks."

"I haven't seen Orcus in months," said Landon. They wouldn't be able to rely on the Parcae for answers. "I say we just pretend like nothing is going to happen, but keep our eyes open. You said the whistle hurts them?"

"I don't know exactly what it does, but the Parcae certainly didn't enjoy it," said Lewis.

"Okay, keep it ready then," said Landon. "I'm gunna run home and get my sword."

Lewis blinked several times. His eyes flicked over to Josie.

"Your what?" asked Josie.

Landon laughed. "My sword. I have a samurai sword. It's for decoration, but it's still sharp."

"Do you know how to use a samurai sword?" asked Josie.

"Stick'em with the pointy end," said Landon.

Josie didn't look impressed.

"What?" asked Landon. "You plan to sass the Agares to death?"

"I plan to not cut my own arm off," said Josie.

Landon laughed again. He left immediately to retrieve the weapon. Lewis and Josie waited until he returned with the sword strapped to his back and a duffle bag strung over his shoulder. He barely managed to stay on his bicycle as he swerved back and forth, steering with only one arm. Inside the duffle bag was a whole knife block's worth of kitchen knives and a set of walkie-talkies.

Having already memorized the next entry, Lewis left the journal behind as they all headed over to Josie's house together to wait for trouble to arrive. Mr. Mays was gone for the day at work by the time they pulled up on their bicycles. Landon immediately began scoping out the house and yard for the most "tactical" positions. He decided the maple tree in the front yard was a great lookout point. With its branches reaching nearly all the way to the roof above the porch it also provided a second route down from Josie's room if they were trapped and needed to go out the window.

Despite Josie's reservations about the samurai sword, she kept a chef's knife and a cleaver within reach at all times.

Lewis left the whistle out over his shirt, and kept a carving knife clutched in his fist.

Come late afternoon, Landon decided he should test out the roof access from Josie's bedroom window. He sat crouched on the overhang while Lewis described all of his past encounters with the Agares and the basilisks in extreme detail.

"What do they use to erase people?" Landon asked. "It's not some innate ability, I assume. That would be strange."

"I honestly have no idea," said Lewis.

"I mean, would it really be any stranger than the Parcae forming portals with their hands?" asked Josie.

"Orcus explained that process to me, once," said Landon. "He let me go through a portal with him one time when I was a kid. The portals are always there, weak spots in the universe, I guess. They use some gland in their brains that manipulates energy fields—makes the portals become active for a moment."

"The only time I saw someone get erased was when they got Mr. Bradley," said Lewis. "The Agares was at some distance, and it had to aim. Missed me and hit him. That's all I know."

"Mr. Bradley? Oh, damn!" exclaimed Landon. "Those bastards… he was a good guy."

"You remember him?" asked Josie.

"Yeah," said Landon. "This isn't my native time stream by about an hour. That's total crap man. Mr. Bradley helped coach the team occasionally. He played ball back in college."

"I just realized something," said Josie. "How are we supposed to know if time freezes? We've all been to the Beyond. All three of us are immune to being frozen!"

Wide-eyed concern was visible on everyone's faces.

"A clock!" said Lewis. "We need a clock with a second hand!"

Josie scrambled over to her bedside table. All she had was a digital clock. The seconds were not displayed.

Lewis put the whistle in his mouth and Landon unsheathed his sword with his good hand. They all stared at the clock, waiting to see if the time would change.

The time, 4:53, sat steady, glowing with red bars. Landon shifted over, watching the door. Lewis stood beside the window, searching outside for any movement. Everything was motionless, but there hadn't been much of a breeze for hours. Josie stayed with the clock, waiting nervously. Lewis's heart was pounding out of his chest.

After about forty seconds of silence, Josie gave a sigh of relief. "It changed," she said.

A car drove by on the street a moment later. Everyone was able to relax again. Lewis helped Landon put away his sword—it was difficult for him to maneuver it with only his left hand.

"We need to find something better," said Landon.

"My grandfather has another clock downstairs that shows seconds," said Josie. "I'll go grab it." She hurried out her door and across the landing. She returned shortly with an analog clock that would do the job much better.

The audible ticks were a constant reassurance that they were still safe.

At five-thirty sharp, the clock stopped.

CHAPTER

19

Erased

A hummingbird fluttering outside the window made Lewis second guess the absence of the clock's ticks. The tiny bird darted across the silent yard, past the still leaves of the maple tree. It must have been one of the animals Mr. Gray ferried through the Beyond. An airplane hung motionless, high in the sky, defying physics.

Landon put a finger to his lips, motioning silence as he crept over behind the closed bedroom door. Josie and Lewis clutched their knives with nervous hands as they stood at the ready.

A creek sounded from downstairs.

"The back door," Josie mouthed.

Landon raised his sword above his head, poised for a downward slash. He looked somewhat ridiculous with one hand wrapped in a sling, but his muscular arm held the sword with a steady intensity.

The silence was deafening as several minutes seemed to go by without any indication of the danger lurking downstairs.

A quiet thud from the stairwell made Lewis's breath catch in his chest. The singular sound was followed by a rhythmic clicking—fingernails on the bannister. Josie's bedroom was the first door at the top of the stairs.

Landon held as still as a statue as the doorknob silently rotated from the outside. The latch clicked against the strike plate and the door slid slowly inwards. Pale fingers appeared one at a time as the hand of an Agares gripped the side of the door and pushed it open about a foot and a half.

Lewis and Josie didn't move a muscle. They were still out of sight from the Agares' position behind the partially opened door.

A long body slid through the gap, arm first.

As soon as Landon had a clear shot he swung his sword down on the exposed forearm of the pale creature. It screeched horribly as its arm flopped to the floor, still twitching, though it was detached from its body.

The Agares crashed the rest of the way through the doorway, sending an arterial spray of red blood across the floor.

Josie pounced like a cat, launching herself onto its back as it stumbled across the room. With her legs wrapped around its middle and knives in both her hands, she hacked and stabbed repeatedly into its soft flesh.

Lewis's jaw dropped.

Josie held tight as the Agares flailed about, trying to throw her off. They bounced around nearly knocking over her makeup table and then smashing into the wall before collapsing down on the bed. Landon and Lewis jumped into the fray, each grabbing hold of one of the creature's remaining lanky limbs. Once subdued, Josie finished it off quickly with a strike of her cleaver to the back of its neck.

Josie stood up, both knives slick with the creature's blood. Her face was splattered and her clothing soaked. Her intense expression was simultaneously terrifying and awe-inspiring.

Landon tossed Lewis a makeup brush that he scooped off the floor. Lewis didn't waste any time as he quickly dipped the brush into the puddle of the creature's blood and scrawled the message across the wall beside the door. When he finished, he turned back around to find Landon prying some sort of metallic device free from where it had been wrapped around the severed arm of the Agares. Landon wrapped it around his own wrist, where it sat coiled like a silver snake with its tip resting at the base of his palm.

Pounding thuds sounded from downstairs. The second Agares was closing in on them.

"We gotta go," said Landon.

A streak of light flashed past the partially open door.

Josie hustled over to the window and threw it open. She climbed out first with Lewis following close behind. Landon pointed his arm with the Agares device wrapped around it towards the door and flexed his hand backwards. A blinding flash shot out of the tip of the coil. A deep, bloodcurdling yell filled the hallway. He hadn't hit anything, but their adversary was not pleased.

Landon aimed at the dead Agares next, sending out another streak of light as he bent his wrist. The body lit up so bright

Lewis had to shield his eyes as he finished climbing onto the roof. A moment later the corpse had ceased to exist. Landon continued to send blast after blast through the doorway, laying down cover fire while Josie and Lewis hopped over to the branch of the maple tree and climbed down into the front yard.

After they were clear, Landon launched himself out the window and onto the roof. He didn't head for the branch, choosing instead to roll down and hop straight onto the lawn. He landed with a pained grunt and came out of it with a limp as he joined Lewis and Josie in running down the street.

Flashes of light streaked over their heads as the remaining Agares fired upon them from the window. They hurried out of sight, cutting through the neighbor's yard. Lewis knew the Agares could move fast. Landon stood no chance at getting away with his limp slowing him down.

They crossed over to the next street and continued moving through the silent world. Up ahead, a police squad car sat frozen in the street. Josie reached it first and ducked down on the far side of the car, breathing heavily. Lewis and Landon joined her when they caught up.

A roar that sounded like a dinosaur echoed in the near distance. The Agares was on the hunt, mounted on a basilisk.

There wasn't enough cover for them to continue running.

The basilisk closed the distance fast. It neared the car, its claws making clicking sounds as it scuttled across the asphalt towards their hiding spot. They hunched down low beside the right rear tire.

The monstrous lizard paused on the other side of the car, its tongue flicking in and out of its gaping mouth, tasting the air. It could sense their proximity.

Suddenly one of Mr. Gray's transplanted crows flew by overhead. The mounted Agares followed the movement, shifting the basilisk towards the front of the cop car.

Lewis placed the tip of the whistle into his mouth and blew it as hard as his lungs and its tiny opening would allow.

The basilisk screeched in pain. It dropped its head, trying to block its ear-holes with its bulky front legs. Time started back up in the same instant. The squad car lurched forward at thirty miles per hour and plowed into the beast's side. The Agares on top crashed into the windshield as the car quickly screeched to a halt.

The police officer climbed out with a confused expression on his face. "What the hell?!" He drew his gun as he inspected the giant reptilian roadkill.

Lewis, Landon, and Josie ran over to see what state the Agares was in. The cop walked back around towards the front of his cruiser as well.

"Watch out," said Landon, "it's dangerous!"

"Stand back, kids," the cop ordered.

With a tinkling of broken glass, the Agares climbed back up onto his feet, standing tall on the hood of the cop car.

The policeman raised his weapon, but a flash of light erased him before he could fire. The gun fell to the asphalt with a bang and a scrape as it slid across the ground.

Landon and Lewis looked at each other. They were both on the same page. Landon rushed out on the right side of the cop car as Lewis dove for the dropped gun.

The Agares turned, lifting his arm to erase Landon. Lewis snatched up the gun and fired again and again until he was out of bullets. The Agares slumped over as several of the shots met their mark. Still alive, the creature snarled at Lewis, but then Landon got his shot off.

The final Agares vanished in a brilliant flash of light.

CHAPTER

20

Fated

A loud pop sounded as a portal delivering Mr. Gray flew apart. The Parca ran frantically down the sidewalk towards them. Mr. Gray bent over when he reached the smashed cop car, leaning on his knees to catch his breath as his chest heaved in and out. "This is bad…" he wheezed. "This is very, very bad!" Everyone stared at Mr. Gray, waiting on bated breath. "Quick! Erase that lizard!" he ordered.

Landon pointed the Agares device at the dead basilisk and flexed his wrist. With another flash of light, the creature's body was no more.

"This is a first…" said Mr. Gray. "Mortals don't just go around erasing Agares!"

Landon had a smug look on his face. "Bro," he muttered with a smile.

Lewis patted him on the back.

"The squad that attacked you has ceased to exist," continued Mr. Gray. "That coil on your arm is now 'checked out' to no one at all! They will notice the discrepancy and figure out which target is missing a squad assignment... you've all just upped your profiles... gone from being somewhere around the three of hearts to the ace of spades!"

"What does that even mean?" asked Landon.

Mr. Gray locked his gaze on the jock. "During the Gulf War, Saddam Hussein was the ace of spades for your people—you've all made *Agares Most Wanted*!"

Lewis and Josie shared a look of concern.

"No one's ever erased an Agares... killed a few, yes, but never erased one." Mr. Gray let out a giddy chuckle. "It's bad," he said with a smile. "But also, oh so tasty of an opportunity." He waved off the confused looks that followed him. "The bad news is they will come at you hard, but the good news is you might stand a chance to win this war! They've no idea what I have planned!"

A second portal opened ahead, just off of the sidewalk. Adeona appeared before them. "They just erased Josie!" she screeched.

Josie made a startled noise, then put her hand up. "I'm still here," she said.

"They didn't do it now," said Adeona, "one year ago, during the summer. I've been monitoring your time stream. This is a splintered timeline now—like a bubble. You only exist here because you aren't in your native time stream, but if you try to go to the Beyond, you won't appear on the other side...."

Mr. Gray turned towards Josie. "This makes sense. You already had the highest profile of the three of you before today, so they would definitely send more squads to erase you when you were younger. We'll have to move fast, before that can happen."

Landon narrowed his eyes. "But didn't it already happen?"

Mr. Gray wrung his hands together. "Yes and no," he said. "We're all in a bubble, as Adeona said, floating down the river of time, waiting to be reabsorbed. Josie's presence here after the demise of her younger-self is what formed the bubble, and she's stuck here now, but the two of you…" he gestured to Landon and Lewis, "you both are free to travel as you wish. You must go back and save Josie!"

A third portal opened in a nearby yard. Orcus soon emerged.

"Sup, Dorkus?" said Landon.

Orcus's eyeballs slid slowly across Landon. "I told you not to call me that." He walked over to Adeona and Mr. Gray, his frown intensifying. "They got him," he said.

"Got who?" asked Landon.

"Same time frame as Josie," said Orcus, ignoring Landon's question.

Mr. Gray nodded stoically. "That makes things more difficult," he said. "It looks like this will have to be a solo mission." He turned towards Lewis. "The Agares erased Landon as well, so it's up to you, alone, to go back and save them."

Landon's eyes grew wide. Orcus walked up to him and patted him on the back of the knee in consolation.

For Lewis, the thought of having to fight more Agares, this time all by himself, was about as dreadful a thought as he could imagine.

"We better go now," said Mr. Gray, "before they get you too."

"What about Prime?" asked Josie. "Don't we need to get him to the Beyond?"

Mr. Gray shook his head. "I mean, yes, that must happen, but not until this bubble is reabsorbed. The other Lewis is in his native time stream… it would kill him to travel out right now while the timeline is still splintered." Mr. Gray opened a new portal for Lewis.

Everything was happening so fast. Lewis looked over at Josie longingly. She stepped forward to offer a hug.

"There is no time!" shouted Mr. Gray. "Go now, before it's too late! If they erase you, you'll be stuck 'til the bubble pops and then none of you will exist!"

"Here, take this!" said Landon, removing the coiled device from his wrist and handing it to Lewis.

Lewis hugged the weapon to his chest as he dove through the portal.

CHAPTER

21

Beyond

Mr. Gray followed Lewis through the portal and then opened up another hole in the universe to send him back in time one full year.

"Don't tell Josie you're from the future—not immediately, anyway," said Mr. Gray. "That sort of thing never goes over very well."

Lewis nodded absently. "You're not going to be coming with me this time, are you?" he asked.

Mr. Gray shook his head. "I must stay here for a while and study the changes that have occurred. Find Josie first, and then Landon. Keep them safe. I'll come back for you when it's appropriate."

Lewis nodded. There was no room for error in the challenges ahead. He thought about his family, blissfully unaware of all the hardships his soul had undergone—both in countless past lives and in his present. If he failed, they would never know it.

They would forget he ever existed, and then would soon follow in his fate along with the rest of the world.

His resolve was unwavering. Even if his universe wasn't at stake, Josie was counting on him. He never knew he had the capacity to fall for someone as hard or fast as he had for Josie. Already, he couldn't imagine his world without her in it. It was like seeing color for the first time. He felt drawn to her as surely as a compass points north.

A moth to a flame.

"Do you know why I chose you to save your species?" asked Mr. Gray as he dragged his bony fingers effortlessly across the rippling opening of the portal, playing with its energy.

Lewis shook his head.

"You're the glue," said Mr. Gray. "The one who holds it all together." He grinned up at Lewis. "No matter what situation I put you in, all the other Chosen in the time stream are always drawn to you. Fate brings you together and their goals become aligned with your own. It's a curious thing."

Lewis raised an inquisitive eyebrow.

"I noticed it long ago when you became best friends with Landon on your first pass at life," Mr. Gray continued. "Without you, the others always flounder, but throw you into the mix and even though it's been a rough ride, here you are, still going strong."

Lewis supposed that was a complement.

"The Agares think you are a simple loose end—an annoyance to be quickly dealt with and forgotten. They are shortsighted. Nona saw your strength, as I do. That's why she gave you that whistle. The Agares think you're the ace of spades, but in reality, you're more than that. You're a wildcard. Now, go get 'em!"

Lewis appreciated the pep talk. It did nothing to ease his anxiety, but it was comforting knowing that a semi-omnipotent being believed in him. Mr. Gray bid him farewell and then sent him on his way.

I'm coming, Josie!

He exhaled sharply as he stepped through the portal to his destiny.

Continue reading for a special preview of:

Into the Beyond

Part III : Fires of Heaven

Paul James Keyes

CHAPTER

1

Trauma

"Five years?" asked Luna, gawking incredulously at Harvey from the passenger seat.

Harvey grimaced slightly. He kept his eyes on the road as he chose a careful response. "I mean… yeah… we still have the debt from the new furnace to pay off, and then the roof is going to need replacing within the next couple of years… it's not cheap."

"It's not a ten year anniversary vacation if you take it thirteen years into the marriage!"

Harvey's eyes flicked over to Luna for a moment, judging the level of irritation visible on her face before returning to the road. "It's not like I don't want to take you places," he said. "I just don't see how we can save up enough for a decent trip when we're living paycheck to paycheck still and have all these big expenses coming up. Airfare alone costs a fortune…."

"You do realize Jo will be fourteen in five years? A teenager already, Harvey. She needs to experience things—go on trips—become more cultured! We always said we didn't want to go to Europe when she was younger because she wouldn't really remember it, but now it's a different excuse. We need to make memories!"

Harvey glanced back at their nine-year-old daughter through the rearview mirror. She was sitting quietly, staring out the window with an absent expression on her face—just watching the snowflakes as they streamed by sideways through the darkness outside the car.

"I don't want to talk about this in front of her," said Harvey. He sighed. "I'm already putting in these extra hours at work. You know that. What would you have me do? Let the roof rot off and blow away before I get it fixed? I want to make memories too, but my first job is literally to keep a roof over our heads."

Luna turned in her seat and placed a hand on Josie's knee. "Josie, honey, could you put your headphones in for a little bit? Mommy and Daddy need to talk about boring adult stuff."

Josie turned towards her mother, and then slowly shifted her head to stare questioningly at the empty seat beside her. It was odd behavior—she couldn't have missed the headphones hanging out of the seat pocket directly in front of her, clearly visible.

Luna reached around awkwardly and retrieved them for Josie. She dangled them out in front of her. "Right here, honey…."

Josie smiled briefly at the empty car seat before turning back towards her mother and accepting the headphones with an outstretched hand. "Adeona says not to fight."

Harvey swerved the car slightly as he glanced back again. "Adeona?" he asked.

"It's her imaginary friend," said Luna. "She's been talking about her for a few weeks now. You'd know that if you ever paid any attention."

The car skidded slightly as Harvey jerked the wheel with a tightened grip. "Which is it? Do you want me to work harder or work less? I can't do both at the same time. You know how drained I get."

"Adeona says—"

"—You act like I'm not working hard every day on my feet too," said Luna. "I'm asking you to be present with Josie. I manage it."

"Adeona says you guys—"

"That's not a fair comparison—"

"ADEONA SAYS you guys shouldn't fight tonight!" Josie yelled over them, finally getting their attention. "She says to remember why you love each other, because each moment is a gift and you shouldn't take it for granted."

Harvey looked at her through the rearview mirror again. Luna craned her head back around too, locking sad eyes upon her daughter for a moment. She gazed over at Harvey next, studying the side of his head. His jaw was clenched tight, fighting back more biting words. His focus remained intent on the winding road ahead, but his eyes soon softened.

They both knew the bickering needed to stop. Josie was sensitive, always reflecting the mood of the room back with a bleeding heart. They usually did better about hiding their occasional fights.

Harvey sighed. "She's right," he admitted. "You girls are my whole world. We're both fighting for the exact same thing—to make our lives better—for our future."

Luna's mouth twitched up into a half-smile. "I'm sorry," she said. "I'm just sick of living for tomorrow. I want it to start now."

"Kiss him," Josie ordered, eyes wide open, staring up at them with the most serious expression a nine-year-old could command.

Luna couldn't squash her smile any longer; their love was too strong. She leaned in slowly and planted a loud, wet kiss on Harvey's cheek, complete with audible kissing sound effect.

Harvey laughed. "One more," he said, shifting his head sideways to present his cheek again. As Luna moved towards him, he quickly turned to face her, forcing their lips to meet in a brief, stolen kiss. Luna wiped her mouth with the back of her hand in feigned disgust.

They were still thirty minutes out from the main highway, heading home from a skiing trip that was intended to refresh their overworked bodies and minds. The weekend had ended up feeling more like a workout than a vacation.

Harvey powered on the radio and flipped through the stations until he found one playing Christmas music. They were supposed to be having fun, after all. The Carpenters' version of *Sleigh Ride* played out through the speakers, interrupted by brief bits of static from the spotty mountain reception. Luna leaned her head over onto Harvey's shoulder, enjoying the dance of the snowdrifts outside. Poofs of white swirled back and forth across the roadway, blustering up through their headlight beams like tiny tornados of snow.

As they rounded a gradual curve into the final downgrade stretch before the lowlands, Josie quietly unbuckled her seatbelt and stood up, hunched awkwardly in the middle of the backseat.

Neither Harvey nor Luna noticed her at first. Josie stood silently with her eyes closed and her arms spread wide, as if she could feel the cold air on the outside of the car rushing over her. Luna was the first to realize that something was amiss. She glanced in the passenger-side mirror and saw an empty seat where Josie should have been. She spun around immediately to see what was going on.

"Josie!" she cried out, shocked by the strange pose. "What are you doing? Sit down!"

Harvey turned his head back as well, unamused by Josie's antics. "That's dangerous!" he cried out. The car swerved again. He whipped back around to face the road, but it was too late. The tires began to skid as the icy shoulder took ahold of the vehicle. Trying to regain control of the slide, Harvey turned the wheel back in the opposite direction, but the car continued to drift slightly off-kilter.

Harvey's knuckles grew white as he clutched the steering wheel with all his might.

Luna screamed.

A bright light filled Josie's vision. The low horn of a semi-truck blared. A moment later, her feet lifted off the seat. She was weightless, floating through the air with an effortless spin. Bits of glass stung like hot oil as they collided with her face. Grinding metal roared behind her in a thundering rumble as the frozen wind blew her hair back wildly. One second she was soaring head over heels, and then the next, the crystalline snowbank had consumed her whole. A plume of fresh powder rose up in a cloud like a trailing wake as she tumbled free of the carnage on the narrow pass.

* * *

Josie sat up in bed, waking with a start. Her whole body was drenched in sweat.

The same damn dream again....

It had repeated often over the last five years.

She knew that night would be with her forever. She would never forget what she had done, nor forgive herself for it. Parts of her wished she could forget the whole night—just erase it from her memory—but she clutched to it all the same. It was her last and most vivid memory of her parents.

Josie rubbed her face, pushing her dampened hair off her forehead. The sounds of the other campers sleeping in the surrounding bunks was disconcerting for a moment before she remembered where she was—Camp Orkila, doing an extended teen summer camp program. The other girls were all mostly fast asleep, faces turned towards the walls as the first gray light of morning came pouring in through the cabin's singular window.

Channie Davis was the exception—she looked like a dark silhouette as she leaned against the windowsill, staring out into the early morning gloom. She turned her head to look back at Josie, but didn't say anything before returning her gaze to the window.

Josie wafted her night-shirt up and down, trying to bring cooler air to her overheated skin. The un-air-conditioned cabin was making her nightmares flair up worse than usual. She could still hear the wind howling in her dark, icy world. The grinding of metal and the crinkling of glass—to her, it was akin to the sound of snapping bones.

That night, her world had changed irreparably.

Today, it would change again.

"There's someone watching our cabin from within the woods," said Channie, her eyes still locked on the window. "He's been standing there since before I woke up."

Josie wasn't sure Channie was speaking to her at first, but after glancing around more thoroughly she realized she was the only other girl awake.

"He's so tall…" said Channie.

Josie blinked several times and rubbed the sleep from her eyes before standing up and joining her at the window. The girl pointed quietly into the dark woods about one-hundred yards out, beyond the cabin's clearing. Josie squinted, searching for a human shape. "I don't see anything," she said.

Channie glanced at her again to check where she was looking, then pointed a little farther to the left. "Right there."

Josie shifted her gaze across the shadows of the tree trunks. A skinny tree, shorter than the rest, leaning slightly against the wind, caught her attention. She narrowed her eyes. It was too tall to be anything but a tree, but it did have an eerie silhouette—it almost looked like it had shoulders and a head…. She scanned her eyes across the region several more times without seeing anything else before her focus returned to the odd shape once again.

Josie continued to watch the shadow in silence with Channie for some time, certain that it was no more than their wild imaginations playing tricks on their eyes… that is… until Channie whimpered a fearful gasp and the too-tall form slowly receded into the forest.

A Note from the Author:

If you enjoyed the novel, I also have another series I'm writing—The Arcadian Complex, featuring my debut novel, Wrought by Fire. The books are a lot longer in that series, as they are aimed at an older audience—a series where I don't hold back on the content. It was and still is a labor of love, and I consider it to be my masterpiece. The first two books are already complete as of this writing, with more to come between Into the Beyond releases. You can read the synopsis of Book 1 on the next page.

Also, please don't forget to leave a **review** online! That, along with telling your friends and family about my books, is the best thing a fan can do to give back. The more attention my novels get, the lower the financial burden of writing them will become (it takes years). I will continue to share my stories, one way or another, because that is what I love to do!

About the Author:

Paul Keyes was born and raised in Washington State between the beautiful waterways of the Puget Sound and the always majestic Cascade Mountains. Fascinated by the political and social workings of the world, he obtained degrees in both creative writing and economics from the University of Washington. In his spare time, he is an experienced pianist and composer, which has helped him bring a heightened sense of rhythm and emotional resonance to his written passages. Over the years, he has traveled everywhere from China to the Mediterranean, soaking in the many diverse cultures and histories. Throughout it all, there is no place he would rather be than back home, drifting on a boat somewhere between the San Juan Islands and his home port of Edmonds.

You can follow Paul on Twitter **@PaulJKeyes**,
TikTok **@PaulJamesKeyes**,
or visit **VergePublishing.org** to become an honorary Chosen!

Also By Paul Keyes:

The Arcadian Complex Series

An Ancient Magic lingers from a Forgotten Era.
Wizards Reign & Terrorize with Godly Powers.

Salvine is sold to a madman who uses her flesh to form a beast with an unquenchable **thirst for blood**. She must do as her master commands—fetch the head of the bearer of the *Mark of Kings*.

Her target, a man plagued with *haunting visions of a destroyed world*, discovers he can bend both man and nature to his will as long as the moon hangs in the sky. The symbol etched into his bicep is more important than he realizes. He is fated to be king, but only if he can survive a perilous journey across lands ruled by powerful tyrants.

When a local boy named Javic discovers the future king on his farm, he doesn't think his luck can possibly get any worse. If only he knew Salvine—the girl he **secretly loves**—is trapped in the mind of one of their hulking stalkers.

An epic tale of magic and mayhem spans a rich world brimming with danger.

You can find the series on Amazon, or visit the website, **ArcadianComplex.com**